Sarah Pratt McLean

Towhead

The Story of a Girl

Sarah Pratt McLean

Towhead
The Story of a Girl

ISBN/EAN: 9783744747783

Printed in Europe, USA, Canada, Australia, Japan

Cover: Foto ©Andreas Hilbeck / pixelio.de

More available books at **www.hansebooks.com**

TOWHEAD

THE STORY OF A GIRL

BY

SALLY PRATT McLEAN
AUTHOR OF "CAPE COD FOLKS"

BOSTON
A. WILLIAMS AND COMPANY
Old Corner Bookstore
1883

WRIGHT & POTTER Printing Co., 18 Post Office Sq.

ELECTROTYPED.

BOSTON STEREOTYPE FOUNDRY,
NO. 4 PEARL STREET.

TO

MARY PAYNE McLEAN.

Contents

TOWHEAD.

CHAPTER I.

MRS. BODURTHA'S PLAN.

MR. BODURTHA, prominent and successful financier on Wall street, prominent pew-holder and alms-giver in a Christian church on Broadway, had a younger brother, Richard by name, who baffled all the virtuous designs of his family in his behalf by seeking a career of his own on the stage.

Mrs. Bodurtha, who, as a discreet and virtuous woman, possessed all the qualities which distinguished her husband as a man, had a younger sister, Lucy, brilliant, impulsive, beautiful — everything, in short, that Mrs. Bodurtha was not.

The young delinquents in these two worthy and aristocratic families further completed their own ruin, and estranged themselves from their families and friends by falling in love with each other, and, finally, a distinct opposition being applied at all

times to the match, by eloping one night from the
country-house of the Bodurthas, in Dymsbury,
Connecticut.   In spite of all, they lived most happily together, and still beloved of the gods, they
died young.

They left one child, Lucy, or " Dick " — as she
came to be called, during the first six happy years
of her life, by the talented and gay who frequented
her father's house.   This little one, Mrs. Bodurtha,
herself left widowed, moved by what she felt to be
a popular sentiment on the subject, as well as
by the expressed opinion of her eminent pastor,
consented at length to receive to her personal
guardianship and care.   But she had no children
of her own ; she had always had a horror of young
children, and the thought of assuming what she
regarded, in this case especially, as so doubtful
and terrible a responsibility, was almost more than
she could bear.   Though a woman of rare self-
confidence ordinarily, and of a keen worldly sense,
in this respect she felt only self-distrust and foreboding ; and as day after day happy little Dick
developed more and more of her mother's fatal
charms of beauty, and of her father's fatal genius,
Mrs. Bodurtha's dread increased.   She was herself

religiously careful to call the child Lucy, but the wicked pet name widely prevailed, and even fell from the lips of Mrs. Bodurtha's pastor during his informal calls, and of her confidential friend and business adviser, Mr. Higgins.

Little Dick displayed no disagreeably precocious traits. She was a perfectly healthy, naughty, natural child, with an innate disposition to charm in her wilful little spirit, with wonderful eyes and hair, and a laugh that showed off certain dazzling hereditary charms of teeth and feature in a manner thoroughly fascinating to the beholder. Not accustomed to being thwarted, she had seldom indulged in an angry or resentful mood ; so that now, when Mrs. Bodurtha found it necessary to apply stern words of admonition and rebuke, little Miss Dick, instead of flying into a passion, gazed at her aunt with such simple incredulous wonder in her lovely eyes, proceeding forthwith to carry out the undaunted designs of her own sweet fancy, that Mrs. Bodurtha, half appalled, half fascinated, and wholly despairing, was moved to bewail the day that ever her sister had brought this fate upon her. That the child would go morally wrong, she was sure ; she would follow in the footsteps of her father and mother, and *she*, wise, strong-willed woman though she was, had only a strange haunting consciousness that she should be all powerless to prevent her.

"I cannot describe my feelings on this subject," Mrs. Bodurtha said to her worthy counsellor, Mr. Higgins. "They take the form of a foreboding, but they are none the less terribly real to me."

She concluded, at last, that she must resort to desperate expedients; for anxiety about little Dick, with her recent trials in the loss of husband and sister, had indeed worn upon her so that she began to languish physically, and her physician imperatively prescribed new scenes, a foreign clime, and freedom from care.

"Since I am not able myself to assume this sweet though terrible responsibility," said Mrs. Bodurtha, "I must, both for the child's sake and my own, steel myself to a separation. Lucy must be given into firmer hands, where there is no danger of yielding to emotions caused by the associations of the past or to too great weariness of the flesh. Unendurable as the trial may be to my own feelings, severe as the discipline may be for my poor dear sister's child, it seems to me that her salvation depends upon it. She must be given to the care of those who will exercise *firm, persistent* and *unyielding* methods of discipline."

Since the time when Mrs. Bodurtha's sister had taken flight, with young Richard, from the house at Dymsbury, Mrs. Bodurtha had never revisited the place. She had not at any time entertained much fondness for the Dymsbury country-house, and that event had deepened the feeling to one of positive dread and dislike. But she had a great respect for her tenant, Deacon Cadmus Pinchon, a man of dignified countenance and sublime stature, who occasionally came to New York to consult with her on business matters connected with the estate. She knew that he had a devout wife, a large family of children, and a creditable number of house servants. Her thoughts, conversant through the Sunday-school literature of her childhood, with certain phases of New England rural and religious life, dwelt long in this emergency upon the good Deacon Cadmus Pinchon family, as, in imagination, she saw it, for the better performance of its duties, divided into orderly ranks and battalions, rising at the sound of a bell, and

retiring punctually, after its useful day, with murmured words of blessing and "good-night."

Ah, if only her mad-spirited little niece could
be immured for a few years with Deacon Cadmus
Pinchon and his wife in this quiet home at
Dymsbury; subdued day by day and led to infant
meditation through the passionless companionship
of hills and flocks! Mrs. Bodurtha consulted with
Mr. Higgins.

Before her unfortunate rencounter with young
Richard, Mrs. Bodurtha's erring sister had been
tacitly promised in marriage to this same Mr.
Higgins, as a partner greatly to be desired for her
on account of his superior years, worldly wisdom,
and irreproachable financial standing. Mr. Higgins had not married, neither had he the appearance of one who bears a life-long disappointment
or who has at any time suffered from an o'er-
mastering blow. His countenance was complacent,
beaming, and affably immoral. And now, when
Mrs. Bodurtha appealed to him in regard to the
training of the child of his former unfaithful love,
he placed his hands together and threw his head
back in a smilingly sentimental mood.

"Ah!" said he, "the little one is puffectly

bewitching! She smiled on me when I came in to-day, Mrs. Bodurtha; that means that she will cut me cruelly to-morrow. She is a puffect little beauty. She will have it all her own way."

"That," said Mrs. Bodurtha, in a tone of only so much grave disapproval as it was proper to assume towards a person of such large financial interests as Mr. Higgins — "*that*, dear Mr. Higgins, is exactly what it is my ponderous duty to try to prevent." She then went on to relate to him her plan for the incarceration of little Miss Bodurtha with the good Deacon Cadmus Pinchon family.

Mr. Higgins listened suavely, tapping his fingers together and smiling. "Excellent!" he murmured at length, in his peculiarly unctuous tone. "Excellent! The—ah—the country is so delightfully healthful, you know."

"Oh, it isn't that," Mrs. Bodurtha sighed. "The child is *extravagantly* healthy. Besides," she added, with almost a touch of asperity in her voice; "the country is the last place to which I should think of sending an ailing child, Mr. Higgins. I am sure the cackling of the hens, in itself, is enough to reduce one to an early grave!"

Mr. Higgins, vastly amused, yet nodded his head in polite acquiescence. ".Excellent!" he again murmured, "excellent!"

"No," Mrs. Bodurtha proceeded; "it is rather that she may have in this worthy Pinchon family the strict and necessary discipline which I, alas! am unable to give. I have seldom seen a person of such grave and dignified demeanor as Deacon Cadmus Pinchon; and his wife, I am informed, is a most devout and exemplary woman. My little niece will be attended by her governess and by an old servant, Excelluna, to whom my sister, in her lifetime, became strangely attached — a poor, faithful drudge, who in her turn is passionately devoted to the child; but, in the station in life which my little niece will probably fill it is as well, perhaps," said Mrs. Bodurtha, "that she should not lose sight of the fact that there are drudges."

Mr. Higgins' countenance shone with sympathy and approval, yet had he been pursuing an amusing train of thought quite his own.

"Speaking of our charming little Dick," he now said, savoring his speech with soft effusions of honeyed laughter; "in ten or a dozen years from now I will myself undertake the burden of her education with the greatest pleasure — I do assure you, my dear Mrs. Bodurtha, with the greatest possible pleasure. Since the mother proved unfaithful, the child may be destined to restore my wounded life. Ah, who knows? Who knows? I should be but sixty then, and no grayer, I presume, than I am now. Stranger things have happened, indeed, stranger things have happened."

Mrs. Bodurtha met the pleasantries of the smiling Crœsus before her with that graciousness which was their due. But, together with the perplexities already tormenting her in regard to the child's training, his words had suggested to her the more awful responsibilities of the future. She resumed, in a tone of intense and troubled seriousness : —

"But, in order that the direction of my niece's future life may be wise and rational, we must seek to lay the proper foundation now. Therefore I have made this plan for her early training ; and, torn from her, as I must be, to seek my own health abroad, I have confidence that, in intrusting her to the care of good Deacon Cadmus Pinchon and his wife, she will be placed under the guidance of stronger and firmer hands than mine.

" By them the poor child's inherited traits of wildness and improvidence will be subdued and rooted out. By them she will be strictly and religiously nurtured. They have, too, a large family of children, and my little niece will have the benefit of that domestic drill which it is always so imperatively necessary in large families to maintain.

"Oh, yes," Mrs. Bodurtha concluded, now with a long-drawn sigh of relief; "in the peaceful and studious retirement of that country home will be laid, I trust, the foundation upon which we may build by and by the graces of a prudent and distinguished womanhood."

CHAPTER II.

THE CLOISTER, DYMSBURY PARK.

THE spring was waking after a gorgeous fashion peculiar to the place, when little Miss Bodurtha came to that particular section of Dymsbury, which, from its extensiveness and general air of inutility, had long been known to the country people thereabouts as *Dymsbury Park*.

Little Miss Bodurtha had never known anything so delightful as the drive from the railway station to Dymsbury Park in Deacon Cadmus Pinchon's family wagon. Change beatific ! from the gloomy upholstery of curtained coaches, and the profound rumble of aristocratic wheels, to a world grown suddenly so illimitable, with its woods, and fields, and mountains ; and a perch on one of the craziest, most enchanting old vehicles that ever rent the pensive country air with its rattlings and groanings and periodic shrieks.

"She needs ilein'," observed Job Trench, gravely. Job Trench was known as the "chore-boy" at Deacon Cadmus Pinchon's, and had been sent to fetch the company from the *dépôt*. "She needs ilein'. The Dekin's fust rate on a hoss trade," he continued, "but I never bet on his wagins."

At this the supercilious look on the face of the German governess, Miss Schomanhaufer, changed to one more resembling dismay ; and Mr. Higgins, who, as little Miss Bodurtha's guardian, was escorting her to her destination, inquired somewhat anxiously :—

"But the wagon is puffectly safe, I presume, my good boy?"

"I tell ye, I don't bet on 'em," the chore-boy replied, a touch of asperity in his tone. "The Dekin might ride from Dam to Bissheby in this 'ere wagin' and not bust a screw, and then ag'in, I've known 'em to fall all ter pieces jest a goin' to mill. I tell ye, I don't bet on 'em. But the Dekin never keeps a *hoss* but what *is* a hoss," he added, reassuringly, after a moment's pause.

Mr. Higgins would have derived a ghastly satisfaction from pursuing the subject with the boy, but Job Trench, having, as he believed, said all that to any fairly sensible mind could be said in regard to a horse and wagon, relapsed into that taciturn silence which was habitual with him.

Mr. Higgins and Miss Schomanhaufer poised themselves in attitudes, studiedly unconscious, and at the same time suggestive of a readiness to leap. But poor old Excelluna, the serving-woman, the "drudge," at little Miss Bodurtha's side, sat perfectly motionless, like one in a happy dream.

Excelluna was gazing through her "fur-offs." This ancient serving-woman, by the way, possessed three pairs of spectacles endowed with such peculiar qualities of vision that she was accustomed to term them, respectively, her "nigh-tos," her "mejums," and her "fur-offs." The first named, it may be said here, she employed for such occasional diversion as she found in reading; the second, for housework and general duty; the third, dearest and last, for such purely æsthetic delights as she derived from the contemplation of the scenery; and now her quaint eyes gazed afar, with such a rapt expression in them, that little Miss Bodurtha was moved to ask, with wondering awe, "Is that where *God* lives, Luny?"

The child had unconsciously solved a growing mystery to Excelluna's mind. The simple creature gazed upon her as though verily she believed the little one inspired. "It are," she answered, almost inaudibly, nodding her head in solemn confirmation of her words. "Yis, ever and a darlin' orphing lamb — for sech I call you — it *are*, and I thank you for them words."

To the imagination of these two, the woman and the child, a shining presence, with feet like lightning, and wings like the wind, parted the glowing sky and stood forth on the mountains. Such a revelation could hardly have brought surprise, indeed, to the child, with her wonderful clear eyes ; still less to the careworn, grief-dimmed orbs of the ancient serving-woman.

Excelluna, who had known Dymsbury Park in its statelier days, did not even note those things upon which the gaze of Mr. Higgins and Miss Schomanhaufer fell with such ironical scrutiny — the tufted, stony, mossgrown condition of the drives, the dazzling profusion of underbrush, the languid attitude of the fences. To her, it was only the smile growing distinct again on a face that she had loved long since.

"Ah, my good boy," said Mr. Higgins to Job Trench, "what does Mr. — ah — Deacon Cadmus Pinchon raise on this — ah — very ornate and elaborate farm ?"

"Sheeps — and cows — and hosses — and live-stock," replied Job Trench, deliberately.

"And what may the *live-stock* be now?" inquired Mr. Higgins.

"Colts," replied Job Trench succinctly, with a touch of malicious triumph in his tone.

"Ah, very good! excellent! excellent!" said Mr. Higgins, laughing slightly. "But I meant particularly what sort of grain does he raise, you know, and — ah — vegetables?"

"I'd like to see ye raise much grain and vegetables with a few sech colts as ourn on the premerses," continued Job Trench, still derisively. "How'ver," he subjoined, returning to his chronic state of profound seriousness, "the Dekin gen'-rally fences in enough for fam'ly use."

To the eyes of the travellers, the trees began to grow scarcer and gigantic in size, and at length, behind a colony of elms, a house loomed up, vast, dim, and mysterious, in the dusk. The sentiments of awe produced by this scene were quickly alleviated by a most grotesque appearance in the doorway. There, framed in the lamp-light which poured through the open space, stood a woman, black-featured as the night, balancing herself airily, first on one foot and then on the other, and grinning with the startling brilliancy of her race; not so much in welcome to the approaching guests, it seemed, as with private relish for some noisy demonstrations which were going on within. Once, there was a lively and complete revolution of this dusky figure on its axis, the sound of a playful fisticuff or two rang out upon the air, and the grin, amplified and beaming beyond measure, returned to meet the gaze of the alighting guests. Excelluna made a desperate search in her pocket for her mejums, but, adjusting her nigh-tos by mistake, the full effect of the vision was overpowering. "Somehow, somewheres," she exclaimed, "I've seen that perdicious emblem of cur'osity before! Vixanna Daw!"

At this, a significant gleam passed over the countenance of the negress in the doorway. In what world, and amid what scenes these two had formerly beheld each other, was not then divulged, but their wanderings had been unspeakable, their experiences vast, and, in the present crisis, their mutual gaze, which betrayed no warmer emotion; was expressive neither of tolerance nor of animosity. "It's a co-ordinance," said Excelluna, solemnly. "That's what it is. It's a **co**-ordinance."

The night was chill, and Vixanna Daw ushered the travellers into a spacious apartment, where a table was spread, and a fire burned on the hearth, and a company of comely and extremely dirty children, reduced to a momentary condition of awe by the advent of the strangers, stared at them open-mouthed. By this time the countenances of Mr. Higgins and Miss Schomanhaufer had assumed an aspect of considerable bewilderment.

"Ah"—said Mr. Higgins, who was short-sighted, and had not detected the Saxon fairness of the children underneath their accidental coating of earth and molasses—"ah"—said he, turning helplessly to Vixanna Daw—"you have a very—a very—ah—elaborate family, Mrs. Pinchon. Where—ah—is Deacon Cadmus Pinchon?"

"Massy sakes alive!" screamed Vixanna, dropping into a chair, and holding her sides in an uncontrollable fit of laughter—"*I* ain't Miss Deacon Cammus Pinchon,—I ain't. O Lawd! O Lawd!" she gasped—"*dis'll* kill me, sho'. Hold onto me, somebody, 'fo' I busts myself— O Lawd! O Lawd!—But I *hab* allas been brought up in berry pious fam'lies, dat's a fac'," she added, assuming with marvellous quickness a composed and reassuring dignity of demeanor. "I nebber libed wid nuffin *less'n* a deacon, 'fo' de Lawd. Gen'ly, it's been ministers; 'casionally a Mefodist or 'Piscopal'—, do—fo' myse'f, I'se mo' inclined to de Presbyteriums."

As Vixanna uttered these words in a truly mellifluous tone of voice, her face was expressive of sentiments the most exclusively orthodox, and having set all the young Pinchons giggling by means of a covert wink, she next eyed them with a long gaze of heart-smitten reproach. "Chilluns," said she, "yo do grieve me so'ly. Can't yo 'member to follow yo ma's 'structions, allas to 'have yo'selves 'fo' company? But I was gwine to tell yo'," she continued to her spell-bound audience, "how de folks all come to be gone.

"Yo' see, dese younguns, dey's allas *some* of 'em up to *sumfin'*, and what should Cammus Junyah take it into his head, dis berry arternoon, but he mus' run away to de Watkinses to play wid dem Watkins chilluns, dat's nuffin' but a po' low fam'ly anyway; and he took his little sister Ruf wid 'im., dat's jes' the mos' gentle and 'missive little gi !

dat ebber was, but she allas min's wat de las' pusson tells her las'. But, Miss Deacon Cammus, agin and agin she's posi'vely fo'bid de chilluns gwine to dem Watkinses to play; and only las' ebenin' I heard her say, 'Whatebber you does, chilluns, don' let me hear o' dat.' So when she 'skivered as dey was gone, she had mejit 'spicions o' wha' dey was, and she sent Vinny Noble — dat's Miss Pinchonses secon' girl," said Vixanna, parenthetically, with an accent of undisguised contempt, "fo' to look 'em up. Fo' dat Vinny Noble she nebber foun' anyfin' yet from mawnin' to sunset — but jest as soon as dey's anyfin' los' she's 'spatched fo' it mejit.

"Wall, co'se she went and co'se she stayed; and bimeby I tol' Miss Deacon Cammus dat *sumfin'* had orter be done, and ef it wan't fo' all de 'sponsibility o' 'spectin' company,' says I, 'I'd go hunt dem chilluns up myse'f.'

"So den Miss Cammus say *she* was a gwine — and Miss Cammus *ain't* a berry fas' walker. She makes a great fuss and stew 'bout gittin' along, Miss Cammus does, but somehow she's one o' dat kin' dat ain't nebber succeeded in gittin' ober much groun'.

"So bimeby, arter she'd been gone a w'ile, Deacon Cammus he come along, an' I tol' him how 'twas, an' says I, ' It's ra'ly gittin' time de case was 'tended to.' So den *he* started off — and Deacon Cammus allas has de bes' o' 'tentions, but I know dat jes' as like as not, 'fo' he git half a dozen rods, he fo'git wat he started fo' ; or ef he should meet somebody ter talk wid on de road, he'd nebber knew how fas' de time flew.

"So bimeby, Gusto Brown, he come along — and *him* I can gen'ly 'pend on ; an' says I, ' De 'mergency's ra'ly gittin' pressin'. So den he say he start right off, and he asks Miss Deacon Cammuses niece — dat's Miss Mollie Ebbelyn, dat's here visitin' — ef she would'n like ter walk along wid 'im, and she says yis,— *so den I gibs 'em all up fo' sho.*"

Now the return of the various members of the erratic Deacon Cadmus Pinchon family was in this wise. First of all, appeared Cadmus Pinchon, Junior, and the demure little Ruth, and straightway proceeded to shine among their brothers and sisters, in such superior distinction of rags and grime as had accrued to them from their more extensive wanderings. Shortly afterward, good Deacon Cadmus and Mrs. Pinchon came back from a fruitless quest, and on discovering their prodigal offspring arrived before them, by no means evinced such choler or indignation as they might naturally have shown on the occasion. Deacon Cadmus Pinchon, majestic of stature and of mien, exhibited an undisturbed benignity of countenance, and Mrs. Pinchon, though flustered with walking, was spiritually calm. It was not until after the worthy couple had been engaged for some moments in amiable, though unhurried conversation with their guests, that Mrs. Cadmus Pinchon's soft brown eye wandered by chance in the direction of the recreant Cadmus Pinchon, Junior. A sudden thought lit up her imagination and she exclaimed, in a round, clear, expostulatory tone that yet lacked any severe element of dispraise : —

"Cadmus Pinchon, how *could* you run away, and grieve your poor dear mother *so* ?"

For answer, Cadmus, Junior, who stood by the grate, kicked an outlying coal with his heel, and slightly lowered his head to hide a grin of voluptuous recollection.

From this hardened culprit, Mrs. Pinchon's gaze instinctively turned to the gentle Ruth.

"Ruthie Pinchon," she exclaimed, "how *could* you run away, and grieve your poor dear mother *so?*"

Ruth's little under lip began to quiver. "There, don't cry, Ruthie dear, mother's own darling," continued Mrs. Pinchon, in the same clear, dispassionate strain; whereat the obedient little Ruth graciously forbore to weep. At the same time Mrs. Pinchon's gaze was withdrawn and became vaguely retrospective, and the deflections of those youthful Pinchons were not again alluded to.

When, at length, Augustus Brown and Mrs. Pinchon's niece, Miss Mollie Evelyn, stepped, glowing and blushing, over the threshold, small cause for wonder was there felt to be in their mutual delay; for Miss Mollie was fair and brown-eyed, like Mrs. Cadmus Pinchon, but the younger woman's eyes were provokingly bright, her cheeks were ravishing with dimples; and Augustus Brown had an air of true distinction, and was withal a model of manly beauty.

In the momentary confusion preceding the disposal of the company at the table, little Miss Bodurtha, who had been drinking in with no end of delight and edification the lively habits of the

Deacon Cadmus Pinchon family, fouud herself accostèd in a loud whisper by Cadmus Pinchon, Junior.

"Hullo, Towhead!" said he, with a good-natured and fraternal air, and yet slightly embarrassed, as having, in this preliminary salutation, yielded somewhat exhaustively to the demands of polite society. "If ye want some fun, ye'd better come out and eat along o' us and Vixy. Vixy's gonter have mush and 'lasses."

Mr. Higgins was beaming gallantly upon Miss Mollie Evelyn, and, in view of the finished manner of the beautiful Augustus Brown, even Miss Schomanhaufer's stern features were relaxing into a smile. Little Miss Bodurtha slipped deftly down from her perch at the side of Deacon Cadmus Pinchon, and followed her youthful benefactor to a board in the rear of the house, less ornate indeed in its furnishing, but suggestive of far superior revelry. There were gathered the little Pinchons all, there was her good Excelluna, there was the delightful Vixanna Daw, and there, in an obscure corner, sat Job Trench, the chore-boy.

Excelluna turned rather sharply on Cadmus Pinchon, Junior. "What do you mean," she exclaimed, "by bringin' *that* child into the kitching?"

"Oh Laws, now," interposed Vixanna Daw, "nebber min' wha' we eats, ef we's only libely and genteel. We's all 'ware o' de fac' dat dis chile's berry han'some and high-bo'n."

"She's a towhead," persisted Cadmus, Junior, in pathetic vindication of his own crown, which glimmered with locks of a hue unmitigably red.

"Yo's a *putty* one to scoff at folks' ha'r, *yo'* is, Cammus Junyah!" retorted Vixanna. "And yo' own head jist a bustin' out wid je'g'ment flame! Dat's w'at it is, cl'ar je'g'ment flame."

But the melancholy Job Trench spoke, from his corner, and an attentive silence prevailed. "She's harnsome," said he, his dull eyes fixed in a sort of joyless fascinated gaze on the golden-haired child:

"She's like the actresses I used to see, when I was an orphan, down to New York."

This old young boy had the look of one who has been early starved and who has seen too much. He, with Lavinia Noble, the "second girl," had been left with good Mr. and Mrs. Pinchon, not long since, by the itinerating vender of an orphan asylum. Job Trench was regarded with that peculiar awe which attaches itself to those who speak seldom and smile never, save it be satirically; and at his sombre recognition of little Miss Bodurtha's superior charms, Excelluna, who had been disposed at first to regard him with disfavor, beamed auspiciously upon him through her mejums.

"I'se sorry not to hab any doxothology said ober dis yer meal," Vixanna remarked incidentally. "'Gusto Brown asks de mos' beautiful doxothology yo' ebber heered, but sence Miss Mollie Ebbelyn come, he took a notion to eat in de odder room, do', 'fo' she come, he was gen'ly 'customed to eat wid me and de children — 'Fo' Mista and Misses Pinchon,' says he, 'dey's berry good folks,' says he, 'but dey aint de libliest company dat ebber was. Dey aint fo'mal 'zac'ly,' says he, 'nor yit dey ain't joc'lar.'"

"Who *is* Agusto Brown?" inquired Excelluna.

"'Wall," replied Vixanna, suddenly assuming a mysterious air; 'he's a 'nigma, dat's what he is. In odder wo'ds, Luny, dey's a myst'ry 'bout 'Gusto Brown. An' I don' min' tellin' *yo*', Luny, w'at 'Gusto Brown's 'fided to me and de chilluns in de mos' strick'es' privacy, dat he's no mo' nor less dan de eldes' son of a forrum juke. 'But I quarrel'd wid de ol' juke, Vixy,' says he, 'wi'ch 'counts fo' my bein' in dis kentry, in sech 'duced succumstances.' And he 'vealed to us his forrum name, dat the name o' dat Jumman gub'ness ain't *nuffin* to it.'"

"And what is Agusto Brown now?" inquired Excelluna, with implicit confidence.

"Wall," said Vixanna Daw, "jes' at pres'n', he's Deacon Cammus Pinchonses hi'd man. But he w'ars de mos' beautiful clo's, and he nebber wu'ks widout glubs on, and he's 'spectin' an apologum from de ol' juke, callin' ob 'im back, ebbery day of his life, 'Gusto Brown is."

Now the good Excelluna revelled in mysteries. Her eyes rolled upon Vixanna Daw with a look of solemn exultation. "I knew there was something extraorjaner about that Agusto Brown, the minute I set eyes on him," said she.

"I don' min' tellin' *yo'*, Luny," continued Vixanna; "dat de reason w'y 'Gusto Brown lef' de ol juke was dis : de ol' juke wan'ed 'Gusto Brown to marry one o' dem forrum prinsusses wid a name dat 'Gusto Brown's hisse'f wasn't *nuffin* to it. 'But I couldn't,' says he. 'Why ?' says I. 'Cos,' says 'Gusto Brown, ' my buzzums wasn't fi'd wid de holy spa'k ob lub.' But, 'tween yo' and me, Luny, it's my 'pinion dat 'Gusto Brown's putty much in lub now wid Miss Mollie Ebbelyn, and she wid him, do she's a mos' dreful case to flirt, Miss Mollie is ; and 'Gusto Brown carries hisse'f so high and ca'm, dey's no tellin' allas w'at his 'motions is. And Miss Mollie's nuffin but de daughter ob a Presbyterium minister : dat ain't no great ketch, to be sho', fo' sech a figga as 'Gusto Brown, and de eldes' son ob a forrum juke ! "

" It appeared to me," said Excelluna, investing this splendid romance with a sudden dark suggestion of tragedy : " it appeared to me jest afore supper, that Mr. Higgins was a makin' up to Mrs. Deking Cadmuses niece, and Miss Shoe-mine-off-ear was a makin' up to Agusto Brown."

"Oh, laws, Luny," exclaimed Vixanna Daw, highly amused. "Yo' ain't had much of de 'spe'rences ob lub, ef you tinks dey's anyfin' to dat. Dey's only jes' a playin' off. *Lub*, Luny," said Vixanna, suddenly wearing an air of supreme significance; "'s like dis yer 'lasses dat I'm a flowin' onto my mush. It's sweet, Luny, but it's 'stremely 'pricious ; it's 'stremely 'pricious."

Vixanna Daw sat at the head of the table and dispensed the steaming oatmeal mush with a long iron spoon, like one who wields a royal though blithe prerogative. The little Pinchons had individual molasses cups. They laughed, they shouted, they dabbled with their fingers in that sweet refection. Little Miss Bodurtha had never been so happy. She suddenly evinced qualities calculated to cope in every instance with those youthful Pinchons. She consumed her food from the palm of her dainty hand. Ripples and peals of laughter fell from her rosy lips. At her delight, tears of sympathetic joy rolled down Excelluna's cheeks. "How you be a enjoyin' of yourself, ever and a darlin' one!" she cried. When, at the height of the frolic, Vixanna Daw laid the robust Cadmus Junior, across her knees and administered a playful dose of discipline, and all the little Pinchons cried, " Spank me too, Vixy!" shrillest and sweetest of all rose the voice of little Miss Bodurtha, " Spank me too, Vixy!"

After the banquet, little Miss Bodurtha was abducted from these charming companions and led into the parlor, from which she was again speedily rescued by the dauntless Cadmus Junior, and introduced to the most marvellous, the most unspeakable wanderings with the little Pinchons, in the cellar, in the garret, through the mysteries of a great gloomy old barn, preceded by Vixanna Daw, with her lantern, and followed by the wondering and helpless Excelluna.

Then there was the enchanting period during which Vixanna peered through an aperture in the floor over the parlor, known as the "dummy hole," and regaled her hearers with a choice, if not veracious, account of what was going on in the room below. Vixanna had besought the privilege of using Excelluna's fur-offs for this purpose, and such an admission of advanced years on her part, as well as the recognition of the subtle qualities of Excelluna's spectacles, had made the latter a more willing votary of her crime. But Vixanna Daw had no need of spectacles. They became entangled in the meshes of her curly hair, while she stretched herself flat on the floor, save for a slight elevation of the heels at one extreme and an immersion of the head in the dummy hole at the other, which order was occasionally reversed, as she recounted to her audience, in a muffled whisper, the result of her observations : —

"It's jes' as I 'spected, chilluns, we's jes' in de nick o' time.   'Gusto Brown an' dat Jumman gub'ness am a settin' on de sofy by de winder, lookin' at de phogertraph a'bums, and Miss Mollie and Mista Higgins, dey's a settin' on de sofy by de grate, flirtin' fit to make yo' ha'r stan' on end.

"And 'Gusto Brown, he's a 'havin' r'al p'lite, but he looks kinda wore out, and once in a w'ile his eyes shoots over dreful to'ds Miss Mollie. But Miss Mollie and Mista Higgins, dey keeps on a flirting fit to make yo' ha'r stan' on end."

" *Where is Deking Cadmus Pinchon ?* " inquired Excelluna, very gravely.

" He's jes' gone out to hunt de chilluns up, to bring 'em in to pra'rs," responded Vixanna.

" And where is *Miss* Deking Cadmus Pinchon ? " inquired Excelluna.

" She's a settin' by de centa-table, readin' the New Yawk R'igious 'Bserver," answered Vixanna.

Gradually Vixanna's head sank lower and lower and lower into the dummy hole. The resurrections became less frequent, and endured for briefer periods of time. " Mista Higgins, he's talkin' in dat voice o' his dat soun's jes' like de po'k a cripsin' in the bottom o' de pot, only mo' sof'. Miss Mollie's a flirtin' drefful.

" Mista Higgins say he's nuffin' but a po' f'l'on bachelum, gwine back to his lonely home in de great city. Don' she tink Miss Mollie gib 'im one kiss to take back wid 'im, when he hab to go back all alone on de midnight owl-train ? —

" Den would she be mo'tally 'fended ef he steal one ? "

Vixanna's head made one brief reappearance and then sank hopelessly from view.

" He'p me up, chilluns ! " she exclaimed weakly at length. " He'p me up, chilluns ! " And, as she rose, she wore an aspect impressively silent and awful.

" Vixanna Daw," slowly ejaculated Excelluna, " did that Mr. Higgins — did he kiss Miss Deking Cadmus Pinchonses niece ? "

" Luny," returned Vixanna Daw, with equal solemnity; " I swa' to de immo'tal Moses, an' ef I was on my dyin' bed I couldn't say no different, dat, *jes' at that p'int I shet my eyes.* Come, chilluns, le's all go down to pra'rs."

When little Miss Bodurtha, denuded of her soiled garments, and washed and arrayed in a beautiful white night-gown at the hands of her faithful Excelluna, sank to sleep that night, her eyelids closed upon a blissful dream of perfect freedom and abounding sweets; of underground passages and dizzy heights surpassing the pride of fairy tales; of giant trees, waving in the moonlight; of beautiful coquettish maidens and disguised foreign potentates; of playfellows innumerable, children fertile in invention, and grown people like children.

But a trouble weighed upon Excelluna's mind, and she could not sleep. From that humble recess in little Miss Bodurtha's apartment, where she was domiciled, the old serving-woman wandered out into the larger room. She cast a loving glance towards the bed where her precious charge lay sleeping, then directed her steps to the window, adjusted her fur-offs, and gazed long and earnestly at the moon. The moon was at its full, and beamed down upon Excelluna with something of the benignity of a human countenance. Excelluna discovered this. As she gazed she grew more and more confident, and at length the pent-up burden of heart began to find expression.

" A deking ! " said Excelluna to the moon. " Yis,

a deking !—and that ain't nothin' aginst nobody, to be sure, neither furthermore nor hereafter it don't not always prove nothing !"

At this the moon seemed to wink down solemnly at Excelluna, as much as to say : "Between you and me and the big elm trees, Excelluna, you've discovered an important truth in nature."

Flattered by this profound and unusual sympathy, Excelluna went on : " Not but what Deking Cadmus Pinchon may be, without doubt, very good-natered and very religioust, and *Miss* Deking Cadmus Pinchon also without doubt the same, but — wall, we all on us have our peculiar rarities — " Excelluna sighed, regarding the moon as though even that splendid creature could not be totally exempt from this world-embracing law — "but it *doos* seem as though some on us was more peculiar raritous than others, and it *doos* seem as though this 'ere Deking Cadmus Pinchon family was the peculiar raritousest family that ever I come in contact with. For there's no denyin' that I've lived with a great many, but my experiences has been heretofore that, in families where the woman went biast the man ginerally went straight ; or ef the man went biast, the woman went straight ; but here it's all biast to biast, as smooth and easy goin' as the sea o' glass ! But I don't know as it's any more of a peculiar rarity than that folks that calls themselves a Christian should go a lookin' of their health in forring parts and leave their sister's only child — poor ever and a darlin' orphing lamb ! — to be strict and religioust brung up in a family that runs biast to biast, and full of nothin' but rampagious young-ones, and forring jukes, and black emblems of cur'osity, the owls of the desert and the pelticoons of the wilderness."

At this the moon seemed fairly to glow with sympathetic indignation from afar.

" How anybody that calls themselves a Christian, and a church-belongin' Christian," continued Excelluna ; "could do sech a thing as that — wall, I'm nothin' but a poor cur'ous creetur, I know. I never was much brung up, nor I never had no advantages to speak on. I wasn't born rich, no, nor I never married rich " — here the moon seemed to be trying, politely, very politely, to hide a faint inclination to smile. Excelluna paused a moment, balanced her spectacles with the nicest degree of precision on the extreme verge of her nose, and gazed scrutinizingly, even severely, at the moon. "I am aweer of the fact," said Excelluna; "that I hain't never married at all. *Marriage*," said Excelluna; "*is like religion;* it had ought to be entered into early. Elst," she gravely and innocently added; "as we grow older, we're more liable to see the folly of it." The moon had resumed its serious aspect and was listening attentively—"But there *air* peculiar-rarities, sech as leaving my own kith and kin', ef I had any—which the Lord knows I haven't—that I hope I never should be liable to."

Excelluna's tone grew pathetic. The moon, though pitiful, was so far off. "Who will guide that purty wanderin' lamb?" she cried, pointing towards the bed. "Who will lead them little wanderin' steps to stand up high and pure where her angeling mother stands? As fur as the East is from the West, so fur was that angeling mother from her as has gone a lookin' of her health in forring parts. When she found me, that had served her father's family years ago, she knowed me. 'Why, it's Luny!' said she, lookin' at me with them eyes o' hern, that never see nothin' on the outside, nor rags, nor humbliness. She

knowed me. 'You must come home, Luny,' she
says. That was her way; she must always have
things brung home. But who will care for hern,
now that she has been took away? Who will
lead them little orphing steps up to that angeling
mother's home?"

The tears were streaming from Excelluna's
eyes. But suddenly, to those poor uplifted eyes,
suddenly to those marvelous fur-offs, the moon
revealed a mystery. And a look crept over
Excelluna's face, not so much startled as it was
first solemn and then full of an exceeding gladness, and the tears continued flowing for very joy,
as she, open-mouthed, stood peering upward.

"It's God!" said Excelluna at length, very
slowly; for she saw palaces and gardens and green
hills and peaceful valleys and a shining road withal,
leading clear down through the branches of the
great elm trees. "It's *God*, that's what it is!
When we was a comin' here, this very night, that
darlin' child says to me, 'Is this where God lives,
Luny?' says she; 'Is this where God lives?' And,
'yis,' says I, 'it is'—not knowin' but greatly
suspectin'—and *now I'm sure on't.* Mebby," said
Excelluna thoughtfully, and as though the idea had

taken hold of her with wonderfully inspiring force —"mebby God 'll do somethin' towards bringin' up that poor darlin' lamb. I never heered of jest sech an insternce before—of its bein' left to Him quite so much entirely to sech an extent — but somehow I ain't afeered for nothin' now. I r'a'ly ain't a mite afeered." And the homely simple face grew happier and happier; and the moon stooped down and kissed the last tear away, and Excelluna went comforted to bed.

Thrice during the night was Excelluna disturbed in her innocent slumbers. She heard noises, noises too of a nature frantic and infernal. The first time that she crept to the window and looked out, "It's the midnight owl-train" she exclaimed, "that Mr. Higgins was a gwine back on." The second time, there was an ominous look on her face and she listened thoughtfully. "It's the wailin's of the—It's wailin's," concluded Excelluna, discreetly —" That's what it is; it's wailin's." The third time, as she stood with attentive ear, peering desperately out into the shadows, a sudden illumination transformed her features and gave place at last to a smile of perfect peace. "It's *cats*," said Excelluna, tranquilly retracing her steps to her couch. "I hope I hain't lived as long as *I* have in this 'ere fightin', squabblin', squallin' world to be kep' awake by *cats!*"

"I might 'a remembered," said Excelluna, turning drowsily on her pillow — "the very first time I set eyes on that Miss Deking Cadmus Pinchon, this very night, says I to myself — 'ef I'm anything of a jedge of human natur',' says I, 'and I think I *be* a something of a sech'—says I, '*that 'ar woman keeps cats.*'"

CHAPTER III.

EXCELLUNA TAKES PAREGORIC.

MR. HIGGINS, with a slight bewilderment in his bland smile, went back to his lonely home in the great city.   Mrs. Bodurtha, with innocent assurance of mind, and with conscience at rest, sailed away to sunny France.   And little Miss Bodurtha was left to the studious aspirations and orderly exercises of Dymsbury Park.

I speak not satirically.   Life is deep.   The Deacon Cadmus Pinchon family, though it might not indeed have borne exclusive witness to that grave official domination implied in the peculiar title of its head, was yet amiable and distinguished in the whole scope of its genius.   Though singularly free from the grinding exactions of mere superficial law and order, its down-sittings and its up-risings, its in-comings and its out-goings, were the result of higher inspirations, that drew their sources from the stars.

Deacon Cadmus Pinchon, tall, broad-shouldered, beneficent of eye, with his noble, bald forehead and long, flowing beard, had a truly imposing and patriarchal aspect. As he sat on the fence, placidly engaged in whittling, that charm which lay ever in the old prophetic grandeur of his presence seemed to invest the humble rails with a peculiar dignity, while his artless occupation became possessed of some deeply mysterious philosophical import. His tones were deep, mellow and impressive. In speaking, he ever began with a slow, wave-like inflection of the voice, a "Wa—al, I do—n't kno—ow," which was believed to be merely the amiable concession of omnipotence ; and when nothing further was added — as not infrequently happened — the listener was still constrained to believe that, if the dry formula of this utterance could be pierced by mortal ken, gems of rare and intrinsic wisdom would be discovered underneath.

In the ordinary nature of events, it would seem that Mrs. Cadmus Pinchon should have been a scold, a vixen, and a shrew, spreading terror and desolation in her path. But herein we behold the unexampled bliss of this singularly gifted family. Mrs. Cadmus had not indeed retired to that soundless philosophic calm which characterized the mental habit of Deacon Cadmus. She was still sometimes to be seen in an attitude of troubled thought, and, though true at heart to her simple religious tenets had now and then been known to advance into the metaphysical realm with all the bold inquisitiveness of irresponsible childhood.   Yet her mental travails were not of the sort calculated to leave their trace in furrows on her placid brow, or to dim the lustre of her soft brown eye. She too said, " I don't know," in tones indefinitely prolonged ; while in respect to material things she maintained ever an attitude as calm, as hopeful and untroubled as the good deacon's own.   There were six little Pinchons ; who, not yet being old enough to discover for themselves those intrinsic qualities most worthy to be imitated in father and mother, had borrowed meanwhile somewhat extensively from more doubtful and alluring sources.   It had been the importunate prayer of Mrs. Pinchon's heart that she might have at least *one* child who should be prematurely devout, a Samuel, original in his devotions, and to be saved but with difficulty from the jaws of early immortalization.

This prayer had not as yet been answered. Never were there six children more vigorously healthy than hers, or who, on being much entreated, offered up their daily orisons with greater reluctance, in tones so revengefully loud and expressive of such a hopeless spiritual sloth. Perhaps some exception should be made in the case of Ruth Pinchon, who, though unideally devoted to her meals, was a little model of obedience, and wavered with equal fondness between the bad and the good.

In the wide latitude of the old house at Dymsbury Park, Augustus Brown shed the lustre of his presence over the stately waste of a former guest-chamber; and it was with no unjustifiable pride that that mysterious youth surveyed in its tall mirrors the reflection of his own chaste features.

Vixanna Daw chose for her domain apartments in an obscure wing of the building, where also, at her dictation, Job Trench and Lavinia Noble remained. This quarter was but dimly illuminated by means of its low, square windows. It had an appearance of surfeit too vague to be designated as disorder, and contained, besides, horrible sem-

blances of ghosts, manufactured by its inmates for
the edification of the little Pinchons, who were too
prone to penetrate into its mysteries.

There were with Vixanna Daw seasons of spiritual
renewal and sublime aspiration ; when, with many
expressions of disgust for the squalor and confusion of her former apartments, and dark innuen-
dos as to the fitness of Job Trench and Lavinia
Noble as moral companions, she would remove
with her personal effects to a part of the house
where wider spaces obtained, and a sunnier out-
look ; but night, alas, always found her back, fully
re-established in her old haunts, and wearing some
indefinable air of elation, as of strange perils
escaped.

The table customs of the Deacon Cadmus Pinchon family were of a delightfully varied and in-
constant nature. At times, Augustus Brown would
wield his knife and fork and flourish his napkin
with inimitable grace at the table with Mr. and
Mrs. Cadmus Pinchon ; at others he would conde-
scend to shine with undiminished brilliance of example in the kitchen, where Vixanna Daw chose
to preside at a board of her own, and where the
meat and bread were supplemented by lively

regalements of wit and laughter. Here sat Job Trench, the silent child of wisdom. Hither resorted the little Pinchons whenever they could compass it.

However wild the distractions of the day, family worship was made to form, somehow, at some time, a part of its revolving orrery. Owing to the vagrant character of Deacon Cadmus Pinchon's spectacles, Augustus Brown usually read the chapter. Those who had once heard could never forget the noble and sincere pathos of the young man's tone ; nor, most conspicuous in the singing of the hymn which followed, Vixanna's weird, sad wail, and the loud, untuned abandonment of Lavinia Noble's measures.

Chapter, hymn and prayer were impartially discussed afterwards by the members of the select coterie in the kitchen, who never allowed themselves to be deterred in the work of honest investigation, either by abstruseness or solemnity of theme : yet these researches, on the whole, were undertaken in no light or carping spirit ; and severe indeed were the rebukes applied by Vixanna Daw, at the occasional glimpses of infidelity afforded in the character of Job Trench.

On the morning after the arrival of little Miss Dick Bodurtha with her retinue at Dymsbury Park, Excelluna noticed that Miss Schomanhaufer looked pale, even ill. Excelluna thought how her own early slumbers had been disturbed by the wailing of the cats.

"Did you sleep well last night, Miss Shoe-mine-off-ear?" she inquired, with a delicate sense of sympathy, as that learned female swept by her on her way through the hall.

"I slept," responded Miss Schomanhaufer, "*miss*erably. I wa*ss* *ss*ickent with frightful and dis*guss*tink nois*ses*. I slept mi*ss*erably."

Excelluna smiled. She had it on her tongue's end to reveal to Miss Schomanhaufer the harmless and insignificant source of all her sufferings, when the governess turned on her abruptly, with an imperative air of inquiry. "Who i*ss* this gentleman?" said she. "This Meester Augustus Brown? Why doe*ss* he stay here? Who i*ss* he?"

Now Excelluna truly admired the beautiful Augustus Brown, and, at the same time, she was perfectly well aware of Miss Schomanhaufer's aristocratic proclivities. She longed to tell the governess that that matchless young man was even

the illustrious son of a foreign duke — but had she
not been bound to secrecy on that point? So she
could only roll her eyes upon her with a deeply
cabalistic meaning, as she placed a finger significantly on her lips.

"Wall, jest at present, Miss Shoe-mine-off-car,"
said she, "jest at *present*, you know — jest at present," said Excelluna with a deprecatory smile, and
weakly delaying to inflict the blow; "he's Deking
Cadmus Pinchonses hired man."

Miss Schomanhaufer did not smile. It was
probably not two hours afterwards that her trunk
was again seen mounted on the rickety farm-
wagon; the gloomy chore-boy held the reins, and
Miss Schomanhaufer sat, pale but determined.
with her face set in the direction of the Dymsbury
railway station.

The surprise of the Deacon Cadmus Pinchon
family at the sudden departure was considerable,
but affected no strange emotions of choler or
dismay. It was believed that Excelluna possessed
the secret. She said nothing, but her look was
unmistakably pregnant. She was determined, for
her part, that nothing should be said to wound the
feelings of poor, beautiful, mysterious Augustus

Brown. So she framed a little conceit of her own, unparalleled at once for delicacy of sentiment and ingenuity of design.

"There's only one thing, Miss Deking Cadmus Pinchon,"— said she, in answer to her easy interrogator — "that I can reveal to you, in regard to Miss Shoe-mine-off-ear's suddint goin' off; and that is, that it *was* cats, Miss Deking Cadmus Pinchon, and then ag'in, it *wa'n't* cats. It *wa'n't*, and then ag'in it *was*." And Excelluna's lips closed mysteriously.

"It *couldn't* have been cats," drawled the soft-hearted Mrs. Pinchon, with almost a touch of indignant remonstrance in her tone.

"No,"— Excelluna answered briefly — "it wa'n't. It wa'n't, Miss Deking Cadmus Pinchon, and then ag'in, it was. It was, and then ag'in it wa'n't; and that is all that I can reveal to you, in regard to that suddint goin' off."

Little Miss Dick's guardian wrote a request that Miss Mollie Evelyn would accept the position so unceremoniously resigned by Miss Schomanhaufer. Miss Mollie's girlish ardor was not in the least daunted in view of so novel an undertaking; besides, she had special reasons for liking to remain at Dymsbury Park. Miss Mollie's instructions began, and were imparted chiefly by means of oral conversations, carried on by the streams and in the woods about Dymsbury Park.

The little Pinchons invariably formed a part of this peripatetic school ; and if its exercises were not of the sort usually prescribed in text-books, but admitted of endless gay diversions, such as climbing among the tree-branches, and wading over the pebbly bottoms of purling brooks, still, my Dick Bodurtha looks back to this beginning of her career in the pursuit of letters with no shadow of regret. To her mind, Augustus Brown is somehow inseparably connected with the picture — Augustus Brown, straying idly over from the corn-field, and doffing his hat, to sit on the bank at Miss Mollie's side. And then the sound of the voices of those two, as it is borne down to the children at their sport below, smacks of no foreign tongue, indeed, albeit it is exceedingly low and sweet.

The children loved Miss Mollie. Her laughing eyes and coquettish airs could play no pranks with them. They found her heart and exulted over her, knowing how weak she was, after all; how tender and womanly, how sweet and unselfish. And although, poor child! she might not have been greatly skilled in imparting to them even such small store of erudition as she herself possessed, she gave to their wild, neglected lives almost the only glimpse they ever had of the yearning mother love. There was no balm for their childish woes like Miss Mollie's gentle voice, no rest for little aching heads like Miss Mollie's breast.

And the children loved Augustus Brown. With quick intuition, they detected in that manly bosom the instincts of the true gentleman, singularly free from admixture with any baser metal; while, as a discourser of rare and unpremeditated romance, there was no denying that he was even more gifted than Miss Mollie herself; and, what was remarkable, considering his position as Deacon Pinchon's hired man, or even as the "son of a foreign duke," he never tripped in the matter of good English, as Miss Mollie frequently did.

The amours of these two cast a glamour of romance over the days, and the secret was sweet to all the children and dependents of the Deacon Cadmus Pinchon family, in that they knew

Augustus Brown to be the happy and full possessor of Miss Mollie's heart.   But why did he not speak?   Miss Mollie would not mind his present forlorn circumstances, she was so kind.   Why did he not speak?—that dear Miss Mollie might be ready, at any hour, to go back with him to the silken splendors of a royal position and the ducal coronet, which could adorn, but not outshine, her lovely brows.   Augustus Brown did not tell his love.   His face took on at times an expression of sadness which would have called for pity, had it not seemed in his case, so supremely interesting.

Excelluna looked troubled in these times; but Excelluna had the air of a victim borne down by more than one weighty consideration.   Her friend, the moon, had gone out in a dark eclipse.   She communed much with herself, often with the dear object of her charge, little Miss Bodurtha—not, generally, little Miss Bodurtha as a substantial presence, visible to the senses.   So varied and wide were Dick's wanderings that Excelluna became accustomed at length to address herself to the intangible essence of that bright creature. And so it was that:—

"Ever and a darlin' orphing lamb," she said, while little Dick was at that very moment far away, wading among the flags, down in the meadow lot —"ever and a darlin' orphing lamb," said Excelluna; "many and much has been the thoughts of late a troublin' of my mind concerning you.

"It has appeared to me of late, ever darlin', that for a child fell nateral heir to as much l'arnin' and governessin' as you was, you air not a gittin' nothin' nowise extry of an eddication. In short, ever darlin', ef it could ever be said of sech a mother's child, you air a gittin' to be the ignoruntest of the ignorunt, and the rampagiousest of the rampagious. Not, ever darlin', but what your natur' is bright to exceedin' and your dispersition most lovingable, but you air not a bein' brung up after that 'ar strict and pioust manner as was thought on by her as has gone a lookin' of her health in forring parts. You most certingly air not. All sech wildness as is and a ridin' of colts bareback you air a learnin' of that black emblem of cur'osity and them little Pinchonses. But, as for sech l'arnin' as was thought on, you air simply, so fur as I can see, not a makin' no pergression whatever.

"I know that I be not myself," continued Excelluna, with pathetic gravity; "much of a perficient in forring langurges. I have always found a considerable to contend with in my own, and though I can ginerally ketch the senst, I am aweer that I am not *always* perfect on the pernunceration. But all sech of readin' and writin' as I know I have taught and shall continue for to teach you. And no denyin' as it's enough for a poor old servin' creetur' like me, but for one fell nateral heir to as much expectations as you was, ever darlin', it r'a'ly seems to me that it is not a goin' to prove nothin' very remarkable of an eddication.

"Folks have got sech an idea of l'arnin' now-a-days," sighed Excelluna, hopelessly; "though, to be sure, there was a good deal made out of *mathtermatics* when *I* was young. Now there was : —

'Jest sixteen yards of *German* surge
For ninety cents had *I*.
How *many* yards of *that* same surge
Will fourteen eagles *buy*.'

"Wall, to be sure, there was *some* that done it. There was Elizabeth Chauncey, that sat next to me in school, that married Holwell Tuller, *she* done it. I for my part, I confess, ever darlin', that no I never done that 'ar example. *Why*, I can't tell. Most certingly did I try, and long was I a committin' of that poultry to my memory. But as for gittin' of that 'ar example, ever darlin', lie I cannot, never could I make no head nor tail on't. I wish that I *had* a been able to, for then I could a teached it to you. But I don't suppose," said Excelluna, sorrowfully, "that even *that* for now-a-days would be considered much of a perficiency in mathtermatics.

"And as for that 'ere strict and religioust bringin' up as you was to have, ever darlin', I have already said that it do not at present appear to be sech as was thought on. Not but what Miss Deking Cadmus Pinchon is one of the best meanin' critters that ever lived, and often has said to me that ef only she could git the children all together in the house and make 'em set still long enough, she'd instruct the Bible to 'em every day. But this 'ere I have observed in respec' to women that keep more than one cat around the house, in respec' to sech women, there is always a *somethin'* wantin'. Sech little religion as I have, ever darlin', which it is mostly, 'Our Father which art in Heving,' I have taught and shall continue for to teach you, but it r'a'ly do not appear to be so much as might be thought liable in a deking's family. Sech, and many more, ever darlin', has been the thoughts a troublin' of my mind concerning you."

Excelluna paused, her eyes rolling peculiarly in their sockets, her forefinger pressed meditatively against her lips.

"I r'a'ly don't see," said this simple troubled soul, at last; "but what it's got to be mostly left to the Lord. Yis, ever darlin', your eddication and your bringin' up has got to be mostly left to the Lord. It's a very remarkable insternce, and I'm kind of oncerting as to the conserkences — but, take it for all in all, this 'ere's a vary puzzlin', mistractful, muxed up sort of a world. Long have I been a tryin' to get it somewhat straightened out, but I don't see as I'm no nearer the end than what I was to the beginning. To be sure, I *may* — I *may*, sometime — but I must say that, at present, the prospects is very jub'ous."

Excelluna shook her head sad'y, and took a small vial from her pocket. It contained an innocent cordial, known as paregoric. Excelluna merely applied the tip of her forefinger delicately to the mouth of the bottle, and then touched her finger lightly to her tongue.

"It ain't a *cure*," said she. "There ain't no cure for sech a mistractful, muxed up state of things, but I have sometimes thought that it was a kind of a perventative." And she replaced the bottle, and walked slowly and thoughtfully away.

CHAPTER IV.

VIXANNA DAW.

VERY tenderly my Dick Bodurtha remembers the guides and instructors of her days at Dymsbury Park.   Not the least tenderly she calls up from the pathetic background of the past that dusky figure which made so vivid an impression on her youthful eyes, and which vanished, too, with such meteor-like abruptness, Vixanna Daw.

This Vixanna wore the mental air of significant centuries, while, physically, she appeared all un-scathed by the hand of the destroyer, Time.   So that a vague opinion prevailed in the Deacon Cadmus Pinchon family that she even possessed a doubtful sort of immortality; this idea was strongest with Excelluna, and amounted, in her case, almost to a conviction.   Through her nigh-tos, through her mejums, through her fur-offs, Excelluna was frequently discovered gazing at Vixanna Daw, the look of intent inquiry on her features gradually yielding to a darkly dawning sentiment of awe.

Vixanna's laugh was musical and gay, her motions expressive of an unstudied airiness. Having, as was her proud boast, lived almost exclusively among families of marked piety, and especially with ministers, her thoughts had naturally been much turned to the contemplation of abstract and religious themes; and, in the controversies on such subjects, which prevailed in the kitchen, Vixanna's tone was not so much that of a crude inquirer after spiritual truth as of one qualified to take a broad and smiling view of the whole theological platform.

"I know," she said; "dat I 'ain't nebber j'ined myse'f to no p'tickler d'nomination, do' I'se berry kindly 'fectioned to 'em all — but de truf is, I'se jes' as kindly 'fectioned to one as I is to anudder, so I gibs 'em all my mos' hearties' doxothology, an', fo' myse'f, I accep's de great gin'ral doctrine ob 'scretion — de great gin'ral doctrine ob 'scretion," — said Vixanna Daw, "as we fin's it, my bredderin, in de 'riginal Greek."

In respect to the conjugal relations, too, Vixanna had reduced her views to a few axioms of almost mathematical clearness and precision. Here, her experience had been, as usual, exhaustive ; and, if her words were to be believed, of an especially infelicitous nature. She spoke of her "husban's," always collectively, always with a shade of sadness ; not so much, it seemed, lamenting the fate of those called untimely to the tomb as an expression of doubtful sentiments towards the still existing, and she was frequently heard to assure Excelluna that there was "one p'int on which she'd fairly 'stinguished herself for 'scretion ; she'd allas libed an ol' maid."

Vixanna had her peculiar delights. She found a secret and lively satisfaction in battling with her dear foe, the horn-bugs, which invaded her apartments in battalions, during the warm nights of June. But her chief enjoyment, perhaps, consisted in walking upon the barn-roof, ascent to which was made easy by a gradated scale of lower buildings adjoining. From this height, her countenance beamed with an indescribable expression of glory attained, and yet with something of a satanic light, as though the act of walking on the roof, though it would seem not in itself immoral, derived its intrinsic zest to Vixanna's mind from the fact

that it was committed while defying the lurid
flames of an avenging conscience.

Vixanna had her specific trials.   Perhaps the
gravest of these was the semi-weekly disentangle-
ment of her locks, which she effected by means of
a fine-tooth-comb.   My Dick well remembers that
the place chosen by Vixanna Daw for the display
of this interesting feature of her toilette was on the
sunny south piazza of the house at Dymsbury
Park, and that, during its performance, she made
no attempt to conceal her sufferings, but gave vent
to many crisp expressions of objurgation as well as
of woe, while a retinue of children, awed but
ever faithful, stood by and regarded the contortions
of their star in silent commiseration.

Those who had seen Vixanna only when, by
reason of some exigency in the affairs of the Deacon Cadmus Pinchon family, she felt called upon
to assume the character of hostess, or on any other
occasion demanding great pomp and dignity of
demeanor, could have little conception of the
buoyancy of which, under certain circumstances,
her nature was capable ; and few were the days, in
the happy calendar of Vixanna's reign, that did
not reveal to my Dick and the little Pinchons,

the delights of some new and marvellous adventure.

But there came a day at last — and Dick may be pardoned, if now, in maturer years, her mind still lingers affectionately, even tearfully, over its grotesque features — there came a day, when good Deacon Cadmus Pinchon and his wife drove off towards the west, in their phaeton, to attend a convention of the potentates of the church, in a town some twenty miles distant; and Augustus Brown and sweet Miss Mollie went off, all happy and unconscious, in the rambling farm-wagon for a drive towards the golden east; and the world of Dymsbury Park was left to Vixanna Daw and her adoring satellites.

As Vixanna then ascended to walk upon the roof of the barn, never had the light which transfigured her countenance appeared at once so baleful, yet so triumphant. Something of the complete ascendency of evil over good in her nature — for the time being, at least — was inferred, when, on descending, she observed confidently, "Chilluns, de Debble's got me, fo' dis day, sho';" and she had the air thereafter of abandoning herself to the behests of that dread though puissant personage with a cheerfulness which had, nevertheless, been drained of its last element of religious hope.

And then, and throughout the scenes which animated the day, the good Excelluna stood by helplessly, and saw visions inscrutable, and penetrated deep into the realm of mysteries ; but found no comfort, neither through her mejums, nor through her nigh-tos, nor through her fur-offs.

My Dick Bodurtha says that later years have held for her few moments of such intense and absorbing interest as when, having covered Vixanna Daw at her own suggestion with the fallen maple leaves which lay by the roadside, she and the little Pinchons concealed themselves behind the fence near by and waited for the victim, pedestrian or charioteer, who should first come down that way. And still fresh in her mind, as though it had been yesterday, is the expression she saw depicted on the faces of those hapless wayfarers, when suddenly, to their amazed and shrinking vision, with dusky arms outspread and glittering teeth agrin, Vixanna Daw shot upward in a giddy vortex of dead leaves.

My Dick will speak in the same fond foolish fashion of the manner in which, on this same eventful day, Vixanna Daw rolled down a long though gentle slope in a barrel. She will be earnestly careful to relate to me all the particulars of that performance; that the barrel was of vast proportions and formerly employed as a reservatory of molasess — which toothsome substance Deacon Cadmus Pinchon was accustomed to purchase for his family in eccentric quantities; that the preliminary act of pushing the barrel up the hill, in which she and the little Pinchons cheerfully participated, was an inspiring though a laborious one; that once, as they paused for breath, the leviathan rolled back over them and sought the base of the hill again; but that she can still hear Vixanna's voice as when, successfully embarked at length on the summit, it pealed forth from the sepulchral depths of the barrel :—

"Now let the wil' herricane roa'
Ag'inst de green ebber-green sho',"

and grew quickly fainter in the distance as that immortal one sped forth on her mad emprise; and that, finally, when they sought her at the bottom of the hill, and she emerged with a countenance dazed but beatific, she observed, looking off into space, and smiling a little absently; " *Chilluns,*

*do you wan' to know what Hebben is ?   It's rollin'
down hill in a barrel."*

Nor was the part which my Dick and the little
Pinchons played in this day's glory wholly a pas-
sive and admiring one.   By the time Vixanna had
supplied the front-yard with the facilities of a
circus, by means of Mrs. Deacon Cadmus Pinchon's clothes-line suspended among the tree
branches, they had aspired to the true spirit of
the occasion, and fairly vied with their illustrious
teacher in life-imperilling manœuvres on the tight-
rope and trapeze.

But the event which gave the day its fatal significance occurred towards the close, although the
sun had not yet disappeared over the western bor-
der ; and Vixanna Daw never thoroughly recovered
from this blow.

There was yet one vehicle left on the Deacon
Cadmus Pinchon premises, an old, paralyzed, huge-
jointed chaise, that had long been cast off from
the active ways of life.   Down in the Broad-brook
meadow grazed a horse that had once been spirited, but, by reason of his extreme old age, curb
and bridle had been for years to him unknown.
This horse and chaise, in a manner known only to

the brain of Vixanna Daw, were combined in one marvellous instrument of flight, and she and her followers, even to the pale and impotent Excelluna, perched themselves thereon.

They were all recovered in due time, my Dick, the little Pinchons, all, and restored to the bosom of the Deacon Cadmus Pinchon family. It was believed that the ancient horse disappeared in the red flame of the setting sun, towards which with one last supreme swift effort he had winged his flight. At all events, he and the vehicle to which he had been harnessed were seen no more.

On realizing the situation after his return from the convention, good Deacon Cadmus Pinchon said "Wa—al," with almost an accent of surprise in the various mild inflections of his voice; and Mrs. Pinchon exclaimed, "The Old Cat'n all!" — "the Old Cat" being the severest expression to which she had ever been known to give expression hitherto.

Vixanna escaped unscathed of body, but as she took up again the homely routine of her daily duties her aspect was characterized by a deep mental gloom. "Chilluns," said she at length to that vaguely sympathetic group; "ef you wan's to know wat's de cause o' my 'spondency lately, I spec's I'se got r'igion. Yes," she repeated hopelessly, "I'se allas been a dreadin' of it, and now I spec's I'se got it sho'."

After this the clouds never exactly lifted from Vixanna's spiritual horizon, though after a time there came a rift in them. "I spec's, chilluns," said she then; "dat do' I'se got r'igion sho', and no help fo't, may be w'at I'se got is only jes' de ordinary sabin' quality, an' not dat pow'ful I had along de fus' spell. It's one thing, chilluns," said Vixanna, significantly; "it's one thing, chilluns, to boas' o' allas habbin' libed in pious fam'lies, and know dat yo's mighty cute at 'scussin' t'ology, and all dem, and it's anudder thing to git dis yer r'al pussonal c'nvincin' r'igion onto yer. And dar's two qualities o' dis yer r'igion, chilluns. Dar's de pow'ful quality dat I had along de fus' spell, and den dar's jes' de ordinary sabin' quality. And I've had my 'spicions lately," said Vixanna, a ray of hope breaking over her long-darkened features; "dat may be w'at I'se got is only jes' de ordinary sabin quality.

"Still, chilluns," she continued, after a pause; "dar's a great deal to conten' for, eben jes' in de sabin' quality.   Now de Debble, he come into my room de odder night a tem'pin' ob me.   He comes in and sets down, and says, he spec's I was turn mighty pious, but dar was some things he reckon I could'n' pray fo' yit, ho'n-bugs, and one thing and anudder, he mentions 'em ober ; and I answers him right up peart dat I *could*, ebery time. An' finally he says dey was *one* thing dat he bet his meet'n-hat I could'n' pray fo' 'em, an' says he, ' Dat's ol' hosses dat ain't got any 'scretion,' says he, an' wunked at me out ob de co'na' ob his eye. But I'd gone so fa' den, chilluns, dat I wasn' gwine ter back out, not ef I cl'ar busted myse'f a lyin', so I speaks up and says dat I *could* pray fo' 'em, *mighty peart*, too, says I.

"Den de Debble, he shook, an' he look cl'ar h'a't-broken, chilluns, he did, an' says he, 'Vixy, yo' was de brightes' jewel in my glory crown.   I done set all my ca'ck'lations on yo', Vixy,' says he, ' but I done 'low I shall hab to gib yo' up.'"   Vixanna drew a long sigh, in which there might have been detected a slight, a very slight, tinge of regret.

As the suns rose and fell, a sinful longing began to grow within Vixanna's breast, to walk once more upon the roof. Sufficient to say, that she struggled against it, but in vain. It haunted her with allurements ever fond and fresh. An October eve beheld her performing that gymnastic feat with a recklessness of gesture and an elasticity of tread never before exhibited on similar occasions. After this, she resigned herself to her fate, with the gloomy consciousness of utter unregeneracy. She said, and there was the unfamiliar gleam of a tear in her wild, dark eye, that "Ri'gion was well enough in its way, but, take it fo' all in all, dey's nuffin' like 'scretion." Gradually she seemed to feel the need of an entire change of scene, and formed vague plans of travel, in which her "husban's" figured somewhat spasmodically as objects of search.

One night, when all the house was still, a dark figure stole noiselessly into the room where the children lay asleep. The slowly waning light of the summer evening revealed its sorrowful attitude, the despondent droop of the thin, black hands. It was Vixy. She sat down and proceeded to sing, in a voice that crept into the children's slumbers like a lullaby from Dreamland, so airy though so mournful was the strain : —

 " De massa ob de sheepfol'.
  Dat guards de sheepfol' bin,
  Look out in de gloomerin' meadows,
  Wha'r de long night rain begin —
  So he call to de hirelin' shepa'd.
  ' Is my sheep, is dey all come in ?'

 " Oh den, says de hirelin' shepa'd;
  ' Dey's some, dey's black and thin,
  And some, dey's po' ol' wedda's :
  But de res', dey's all brung in.
  But de res', dey's all brung in.'

 " Den de massa ob de sheepfol',
  Dat guards de sheepfol' bin,
  Goes down in de gloomerin' meadows.
  Wha'r de long night rain begin — .
  So he le' down de ba's ob de sheepfol'.
  Callin' sof', ' Come in.   Come in.'
  Callin' sof', ' Come in.   Come in.'

 " Den up t'ro' de gloomerin' meadows.
  T'ro' de col' night rain and win',
  And up t'ro' de gloomerin' rain-paf',
  Wha'r de sleet fa' pie'cin' thin,
  De po' los' sheep ob de sheepfol',
  Dey all comes gadderin' in.
  De po' los' sheep ob de sheepfol',
  Dey all comes gadderin' in."

At the close, Vixanna shook her head, and said,
in a broken, pitiful tone of voice, " Dey's nuffin' to
de wo'ds; oh, dey's nuffin' to de wo'ds.   De
music's hebbenly, but dey's nuffin' to de wo'ds."
However, she sang them over again, and once

again, and then, rising and groping out blindly before her with her hands, for the room had grown quite dark, she repeated them softly to herself, and muttered, with a sobbing laugh, in undertone, " Dey's nuffin' to de wo'ds. De music's hebbenly, but dey's nuffin' to de wo'ds." She stumbled a little at the door, and turned with a quick deprecating gesture, but the even breathing of the children fell undisturbed upon her ear. Very slowly she turned her face and groped her way down the stairs.

The next morning, the bed in Vixy's room appeared neat and undisturbed. The room had been carefully swept and garnished. The high-backed wooden chair had been set with punctilious neatness against the wall. By its side, with an almost human appeal in its reclining attitude, stood the feather-duster with which Vixy had been wont to battle with the horn-bugs — but Vixy had gone away.

CHAPTER V.

JOB TRENCH, THE CHORE-BOY, AND BEAUTIFUL AUGUSTUS BROWN.

DICK mourned for Vixanna Daw; and when the leaves had all fallen from the trees, and the wind wailed about the house, and the great front gate, touched by no human hand, swung open on its hinges, she listened eagerly for the tread of the lithe feet that never came back to Dymsbury Park.

But the winter days came and they were full of pleasures. Then had the good Excelluna less frequent recourse to her fur-offs, while she made still vaster researches in the metaphysical realm open to her mejums and her nigh-tos. Much she pondered her Bible, but was even more frequently discovered perusing those pages which, to her mind, constituted the flower of all human productions, the gem of all literature, "Fox's Book of Martyrs."

"Whoever," Excelluna had been heard to say, with solemn enthusiasm; "whoever writ that book, or through whom or by whom that most wondrous book was wrat, is to me unbeknownst, but I hev my suspicions" — and here her forefinger sought her lips and her eyes rolled upon her listener with that look of deeply hidden meaning : but she never revealed who, to her mind, had committed the unparalleled deed, and had once been known to treat a suggestion of Vixanna Daw's, that, "Perhaps de ol' fox hisse'f writ it," with justly contemptuous disdain.

Excelluna's Book of Martyrs was an illustrated edition, and it was a never-failing source of wonder to those who knew her, how that exquisitely tender and compassionate soul could devour its ghastly contents with such evident relish, even with an expression of positive delectation. There was one picture especially, representing the writhings of a victim impaled, over which Excelluna was accustomed to gloat with an unaccountable fondness, and sometimes fell asleep with a look of awful entertainment on her features, and a finger glued affectionately to the blood-curdling spectacle. Or, amid scenes of mirth and merry-making, while

Dick and the little Pinchons revelled in the odor of parching corn and cooling taffy, from that dim corner where Excelluna sat a voice would be heard to arise, as she, in her utter abstraction, jubilantly announced aloud the headings of the awful chronicle: "Four mart-yi-ers plunged in a bag of vent-yu-mous snakes!" "Seven mart-yi-ers simon-tail-i-ously kill-ed in co-old blood!" And yet Excelluna was constitutionally incapable of killing a fly. She had a pathetic yearning towards all the weak and suffering in nature, and saw a face of human sorrow in every stricken flower.

It was with another spring, that, to the hearty, rollicking life at Dymsbury Park, there came for my Dick a wonderful shadow and the echo of a deeper meaning. Among the places expressly forbidden to Dick and the little Pinchons, and — though not directly in consequence of the threat, perhaps, — at all events, most resorted to by them, was a ledge, a half mile or more distant from the house, known as "Craggy Head." On the occasions when they surreptitiously fled to this fascinating spot, Job Trench, guided by some mysterious instinct, as they believed, invariably discovered and followed them — not for sport, — poor Job was not subject to such childish weaknesses. He was the one weary, plodding member of the house at Dymsbury Park, a character entirely self-imposed, and sustained in the face of all discouragements ; and he followed the children in the same joyless, faithful, mechanical fashion that he was accustomed to perform his ordinary duties about the house and farm.

"There's no use in tellin' on 'em to the folks," Job observed to Excelluna, who approached nearest to him in point of sympathy ; "they talk to 'em, but it don't hender their goin' thar jest the same. And you tag around after 'em patient enough, but the little imps makes out to dodge ye, whenever they has a mind to ; and by and by," said Job Trench, referring to young Dick Bodurtha with a dull matter-of-fact recognition of worldly estimates — "by and by, there'll be one of these rich-family high-toned ones gone plump headlong over that precerpice." So Job Trench kept a sharp eye on all the paths that led to "Craggy Head."

One day, as the children amused themselves by throwing stones over the ledge, and Job Trench sat gloomily by, Dick suddenly parted from the rest of the group, and ere a hand could be stretched out to detain her, with a wild shout of glee the fearless, thoughtless child had clambered out upon the branches of a dwarf tree that grew sheer out from the face of the precipice. But return looked difficult, and the shrub bent dangerously under the child's light weight.

"I've been expectin' it," said Job Trench then, in a dull, slow tone of resignation; but, so quick was he in action that not the first look of startled wonder had crept into the eyes of the child, hanging there below, ere he had climbed out to her relief. Then, as Cadmus Pinchon's sturdy arms received her from above, the light tree broke beneath Job Trench's straining feet and he fell.

It was good Deacon Cadmus Pinchon himself who carried the poor chore-boy home in his arms; and they laid him on a white bed in a great chamber, and were very tender and pitiful over him, but Job Trench's wounds had gone too deep for cure, and life with him, said the Dymsbury doctor, was a matter of hours rather than days. His face, always an uncanny one, looked positively ugly as it lay against the pillows, stupid and frozen in its helpless expression of agony. Opening his eyes occasionally, in brief moments of consciousness, it was with a startled, anxious look and incoherent mutterings of alarm, until he caught sight of Dick Bodurtha's sunny head in the room. Then, as if realizing his duty done, his eyes would rest upon her — rest, but without a smile, and fade out, wearily satisfied, in the light of her golden hair.

Excelluna's eyes were dim and red with weeping. "I don't worry none about his 'tarnal welfare," she sobbed, in answer to some remark of Mrs. Cadmus Pinchon's. " He never talked much — only, when the time come, he went and *did* it. But, to think, Miss Deking Cadmus, how I have been a worryin' because it seemed as though there wa'n't a bein' no eddication and no lessons teached! And least of all I didn't look for no lesson from that poor low-borned looked-shy-of thing! But he has teached a lesson, Miss Deking Cadmus, as all the schoolin' and governessin' in the world 'll never come up to! No, Miss Deking, I don't worry none about *his* 'tarnal welfare. More than that, the very first night I come here, I had it in a revelation as God lived in these parts — and I shan't never disbelieve on't now — never, as long as I live !"

But late in the second day, Job Trench's pain-benumbed features relaxed into an expression, intelligent, and almost fine. He spoke distinctly and with his usual gravity. "The sun's a-comin up over them poplars," he said, looking very intently before him ; "I must drive the cows to pasture." He made a patient effort to rise, but fell back weakly.

"No, poor boy," exclaimed Mrs. Pinchon, with an unusual degree of unction in her clear, monotonous voice ; "it's night, poor boy ! It's growing night."

Excelluna lifted her finger in warning. "Hush ! Miss Deking Pinchon," she whispered, solemnly. "There *be* lands, Miss Pinchon, where it's day when it's night here ; and there *be* lands, Miss Pinchon, where *there ain't no night !* "

But Job Trench had not heard. His grave, unseeing eyes wandered over the figures in that shadowy room to the window that looked off toward the east, and rested there, forever seeing.

So there crept into the life at Dymsbury Park the wonderful mysterious shadow of the grave — a shadow more wonderful than sad, since the poor chore-boy's dreary face reflected such strange prescience of an unearthly dawn. And often now,

from the familiar melody of birds and brooks about
Dymsbury Park, my Dick Bodurtha turns and
listens : for, down among the meadow grasses, as
they darken, swept by the light breath of a summer cloud, she hears a sound like a flute note,
plaintive and sweet and low, that rises ever fainter
and more clear; and she tells Excelluna — and
Excelluna listens, with a rapt face and her ear bent
to the earth, and a look of unutterable enlighten-
ment creeps over her features ; for, yes, she hears
it, too.

It was not long after Job Trench's death that :
"I will tell you a story," said Augustus Brown.
"It is a story which Deacon Pinchon and Mrs.
Pinchon should hear, too"—for it chanced that
the family was all gathered then in the long sitting-room. "I beg that you will all give me a
few moments of your earnest attention."

The children, silenced by this announcement,
hung breathless and expectant on the lips of their
oracle. But what meant that hard and unusual
resolution in the speaker's tone, and the extreme
pallor which overspread his countenance ? Beautiful Augustus Brown hesitated ; his hand, thrown
lightly on the back of a chair, trembled ; his eyes

gleamed with an unsteady light ; and for once, he whose speech had ever been fluent and golden, seemed to find no words wherewith to express his meaning.

A terrible premonition, like a chill wave, crept over Excelluna's soul. Since Job Trench's death, she had stood in a sort of awe of herself and all the inhabitants of Dymsbury Park, regarding it as the peculiar seat of Divinity, and knowing not in what form He might next be manifested. And now, as she looked upon Augustus Brown's suffering face, she would fain have made something lighter of it, and could not bear that it should be, as she divined, beyond the reach of remedy. Seizing her Book of Martyrs, she rushed forward and whispered eagerly in his ear : "Take it, A'gusto Brown. Present it to her ! I know not what has been the difference betwixt you and Miss Mollie, but sech a gift as this, A'gusto Brown, I am certing she will not re-fuse. Whatever has been the difference," said Excelluna, holding out her precious volume with one last fond clinging grasp ; " present this to her, A'gusto Brown, and all may yit be well."

Very kindly and sadly poor Augustus Brown smiled upon Excelluna and shook his head.

Excelluna gasped for breath. The tears came. She made a desperate plunge into her pocket and brought forth her beloved bottle of paregoric. "Take it!" she murmured quickly, in an almost inaudible tone; "take it! A'gusto Brown. I have generally found it serficient to tetch the tongue, but there might be cases, A'gusto Brown — there might be cases in which I would advise a teaspoonful. It ain't a cure — oh, I know there ain't no cure, A'gusto Brown, but I have sometimes thought that it was a kind of a perventative."

But when Augustus Brown shook his head again, looking so kindly and sadly upon Excelluna, the good soul replaced her treasures with the look of one stricken to the heart, and turned hopelessly away.

"It is a true story," Augustus Brown then went on. "It is not long. There was a lad — his true name is Wilfred Knight — born in England of respectable parents. They acquired wealth; they lived splendidly and lavished favors upon him, their only child. He had tutors and travelled whithersoever he would. It was, as they believed, through the treachery of another firm, his father's fortune fell with a crash. The wretched man became insane;

the mother died. The lad was maddened with grief and terror. He had been educated, but not as one who should ever need to employ any craft or profession of his own. His moral sense, God knows, was crude. He was adrift on the world — he found companions enough. He had not cared for grovelling vices hitherto; now he drank wildly; he lay one night, drunk, on the street.

"One night they planned a robbery, he and his companions. It was on the bank through whose means he believed his father had been defrauded. He was drunk — the most reckless and adventuresome of them all. They accomplished the feat with mad daring, and escaped. Afterwards, one night, he heard them talking as though he might prove troublesome to them. He fled secretly; he had none of the booty. He escaped to America. Later, he learned through the newspapers that the three had been captured. They had given evidence against him; search was being made for him. He wandered down into Connecticut. He was penniless; he let himself to a good man as a farm-laborer. They never discovered him.

"In that quiet, sheltered spot," continued Augustus Brown, with greater composure of voice as his face grew gradually more and more like the face of one dead; "the anger, the madness, the wretched passion faded out of his soul. He even had something of the poet in his nature. Fields, streams, and woods grew conscious and dear to him. He developed a faculty for dreaming. But *conscience* was not yet awakened in him; that was not till *she* came, the pure, sweet girl whose innocent trust subdued the lingering trait of vice in his nature, whose generous love conquered the selfishness of his passion and transformed it into a devotion, noble, and pure, and worthy" — Augustus Brown's eyes flashed light and his voice rang out clearly — "of *any* man who should dare to say he loves her!

"And though the love which woke his better nature into life could not then spare her who had inspired it, he would not, though he desired her above all things, cause her, unsuspecting, to assume the disgrace of his name. Yet he shrank from revealing the dark past. He hesitated, heartbroken for her and for himself. He has resolved to hesitate no longer, neither to conceal nor fly from his disgrace. He will return to England, submit himself to the authorities, suffer the penalty for his crime.   So that, if he ever start again in the world — if he ever shall, God knows — it shall be fairly in the sight of man, and well in the sight of Him whom, above man, he has learned to honor.

"My friends," said beautiful Augustus Brown, rising, white but calm, and with a perfect command of voice and gesture, as his eyes rested steadfastly on good Mr. and Mrs. Pinchon, "I thank you for your unworldly goodness.   Believe me, if I had been made a subject of prayer amongst all the churches in Christendom, if I had been made in these two years to suffer the tortures of the rack, it could not have awakened in me the infinite sorrow and remorse which I have experienced in this gentle, unsuspecting household. Believe me, too, when I tell you that I have played no double part here.   The life into which you have permitted me to enter, has been with me only the deepest expression of the heart.   I thank you for all.   I pray your forgiveness for all.   I bid you farewell.

"Mary," said Augustus Brown, turning to sweet Miss Mollie, whom they all loved, as she sat with her face bowed in her hands ; " here, in the presence of those before whom you have been so grieved and wronged "—but here a look of unbearable agony crossed his face, and he forgot that there were any save they two in the room as he fell on his knees before her. A pathos deeper than that of tears crept into his voice.

"Dearest, the heart that was won to you, in the sunny unawakened days when first I knew you, was not a fickle one. But the heart that you woke to a better life, the sweet, terrible struggle of faith and repentance, and to the anguish of love that, for love's sake, must forego the dear possession of its object, holds you, loves you, cherishes you for all time. Yet your life should be a happy one, free from taint or shadow. Let the past, blameless to you as to an angel, fade from your mind. But oh, my lost love, before I go away from you forever, though you never look at me again, reach out your hand and touch me,—touch me once more in token of forgiveness!"

When, at those words, dear Miss Mollie, who had ceased weeping, lifted up her face, they saw that it had grown in so few moments to be a woman's face, tender, and true, and strong. And they saw her stoop down with infinite love and compassion towards him who knelt there at her feet, and lift his sorrowful, stricken head and fold it to her bosom.

Ah, well — I who write this know that Augustus Brown will come back again with honor and wealth, when, for his hard-earned reputation, the gray has crept early into his hair; and sweet Miss Mollie will wait for him, while a beauty deeper than that of the dimples chastens her lovely face. But the song of the thrush in the lone Dymsbury woods, at evening, was not sadder than that parting.

Deacon Cadmus Pinchon felt sensibly the loss of the handsomest, most intelligent and helpful, hired man that he had ever known. For, though Augustus Brown had devoted some hours to æsthetic pursuits and to love-making, the sagacity and wit displayed in his moments of toil had caused his services to assume a peculiar value. As for Mrs. Pinchon, she had found the story a strangely disconnected and incomprehensible one. She never really understood why Augustus Brown went away, and, at any subsequent mention of his name, her eyes were seen to assume their vaguely thoughtful, introverted expression.

But Excelluna, poor Excelluna, knew and understood with that truest, deepest intuition of the heart. Long were her eyelids swollen with weeping, yet wore she, withal, the calm of a transcendent triumph."

"Ever and a darlin'," said she to the invisible spirit of her wandering charge; "it's all well enough, this bein' of a forring juke, but there *is* things as is more exceedingly betterer by fur, even than bein' of a forring juke, and that beautiful A'gusto Brown discovered what it was. And, ever darlin', don't let me never say no more impitous words about your bein' not brung up and about you not gettin' nothin' nowise extry of an eddication ; for, in revelation after revelation, have I been teached that it ain't no small thing to be brung up in the same place along o' God."

And now there comes another voice to the wild beauty of Dymsbury Park ; for when the west wind calls shrilly from over the mountains, Dick listens, and she hears a sound like a bugle note, jubilant and sweet, and that rises ever fainter and more clear ; and she has no need to tell Excelluna, for Excelluna, listening with hushed breath, nods her head in solemn confirmation.

CHAPTER VI.

AT SCHOOL IN THE SADDLE.

AFTER Miss Mollie Evelyn went to her home, the air of Dymsbury Park proved unfavorable to governesses. There came those skilled in all knowledge, and conversant with all forms of etiquette, but none who possessed the happy secret of sweet Miss Mollie's method. These erudite females remained at Dymsbury Park for periods of time uniformly brief, and Mr. Higgins was on this account reduced to a condition of much perplexity, almost of despair.

He felt obliged at length, though regretfully, on account of the lady's low physical condition, to write to Dick's aunt, Mrs. Bodurtha, that there seemed to be a sad inability on the part of modern governesses to adapt themselves to the evidently happy state of things at Dymsbury Park; that good Deacon Cadmus Pinchon and his wife were, as she had divined, the most amiable and estimable people ; that little Miss Dick seemed supremely content with the life at Dymsbury, and to derive unbounded delight from the companionship of the little Pinchons ; that, in short, the only difficulty in carrying out the plan of her youthful education seemed to be a fatal incompatibility in the nature of governesses.

Mrs. Bodurtha replied that she had sometimes feared the worst ; that nothing but the warning of her physicians could have prevented her from taking personal charge of her poor dear sister's poor dear wilful child ; that she was not recovering her wasted energies with the rapidity she had hoped for from her stay abroad, but that as soon as it was possible for her to do so she should return to assume the care of little Miss Bodurtha.

At this last clause, Excelluna was again transformed into a bitter fountain of tears, and Dick clenched her fists in hopeful defiance. A few weeks later, news came that Mrs. Bodurtha was prostrated with a fever, from which it was likely to be long ere she would recover, and still longer ere she would be permitted to return to take up any new burdens and responsibilities ; at which painful intelligence, it must be said, the tumult awakened in the bosom of my Dick and that ancient serving-woman was lulled into a remorseless calm.

Meanwhile, Cadmus Pinchon Junior, who had become a sturdy, though bookless, attendant at the district school, lured Dick Bodurtha thither by means of a glowing and graphic description of the diversions to be found at that humble seat of learning. Dick found the entertainments of the place, indeed, rich and varied, but hardly sufficient to compensate for a certain pungent lack of ventilation in the school-room; so that, after a brief trial, although she was frequently on hand to participate in the out-of-door sports of the children at recess, she concluded to forego entirely the delights of the interior.

Swiftly the happy months flew by; and, as one after another the little Pinchons became matriculated at the district school, and her companions, Ruth and Cadmus, passed from that to the academy, wilful Dick took up her solitary enjoyments. There was a horse in the "star window" stable of the old barn that had gradually come to be regarded as her peculiar property, — an animal, not of the arch-necked and flowing-maned species, but

possessing qualities suggestive of an adaptability
to great practical speed. Dick had first conceived
an affection for this gaunt, long-limbed brute when
it had been a sickly, unpromising colt in the
meadows, and she had there surreptitiously minis-
tered to its woes; and she now disdained all good
Deacon Cadmus Pinchon's offers of sleeker quad-
rupeds in exchange, as promising but a tame sub-
stitute for the racking trot and furious gallop of her
favorite, ugly steed. In the garret, among the
relics of her family, she found saddle and bridle,
and she purchased a velvet jockey-cap that shaded
her handsome eyes and crested with extreme jaun-
tiness her shock of loose, light hair. Then she
had her row-boat on the river, and she could swim,
and when winter changed the form of one dear
element, she vied gloriously with the Dymsbury
lads on skates. The gaunt, fleet horse she rode
through all seasons. In sun or wind or rain her
face never lost its exquisite clearness of complex-
ion, but the small hands that tugged, for the most
part ungloved, at the bridle or the oar, became
brown, and marked with numerous historic and
descriptive scars.

Sometimes Dick sighed for feats of companionship, and went drowning "woodchucks" out of their holes, or launching shaky rafts on the river with some bright lads, habitual truants from the Dymsbury academy, towards whom her manner was frank, unembarrassed, and fraternal. These lads admired her. She was the actual heroine of the romances over which they pored most eagerly — an orphan, dashing, handsome, fearless; there was no feminine glory in the thrilling tales of the Virginian backwoods or western frontier life to surpass her, and they tendered her the first valiant homage and devotion of boyhood.

In her wild life, Dick was careful to fortify herself mentally against the shafts of learned ridicule. There was a perch in the cherry-trees, and for rainy days a loft in the old barn, which could testify to fleeting wafts of the musty atmosphere of those moth-eaten volumes which Dick brought thither from her grandfather's library, and to which she gave, indeed, desultory moments of application, catching here and there stupendous notions of the genesis of worlds and of the great economy of the heavens, detached statements from vast systems of ethics and philosophy; and when Cadmus Junior, in whose case the familiarity born of long acquaintance precluded the exercise of gallantry, taunted her with her ignorance, she hurled back at him fragments of theories so abstruse and words of such ponderous sound, that he was forced to contemplate in abashed silence the insignificance of his own attainments.

Possibly it was owing to the theological works in which she dabbled among others, but Dick conceived at this time the idea of being a woman-preacher. She indited at odd moments some very inky sermons, and delivered them with great ornateness of tone and gesture, the good Excelluna constituting her sole but ever faithful and attentive audience. Sometimes Excelluna augmented the importance of the occasion by wresting a "voluntary" from the cracked organs of her concertina, an instrument the full enjoyment of which had ever been denied her among civilized circles, but to which, especially when accompanied by Excelluna's voice, Dick Bodurtha listened with undeniable pleasure. But if Cadmus Pinchon Junior, had been awed by the display of Dick's unusual attainments, what, as she listened, were the emotions of the solitary, the humble, the adoring Excelluna? She wept and she smiled ; she wondered and she gasped for breath.

"And I have been a worryin' about your bring-in' up, ever and a darlin'!" she exclaimed, in satirical accents. "Yis, *I, I* have been a worryin' about your eddication — and in all the ministers that ever I have heard preach, never have I heard words more long-soundin' or more beautiful than has fell from your lips to-day. In how many and a many more revelations," she continued, with intense self-scorn; "will it have to be impressed onto me that you are a bein' brung up in the same place with God!"

In her occasional calm and philosophical moments Dick found a singular fascination in the society of the ancient serving-woman. "Luny," said the girl solemnly, on one occasion, proceeding to draw forthwith from her copious vocabulary, "You seem to me to be absolutely simple and yet infinitely profound."

"Ever and a darlin'," said Excelluna, by no means understanding the significance of those words, but impressed beyond measure by their ponderous sound; "though I fear that I have not yet attained unto sech, it has been and shall ever be my most earnest prayer that I may become so." And the lingering music of the phrase repeated itself to her ear in cadences ever more solemn and sedate.

It chanced, one spring time, that Deacon Cadmus Pinchon gave to these two their choice of any two of the young lambs in his flock. Excelluna's affections yearned instinctively over one of a triple birth, the puniest of all, bleating and miserable and forsaken of its mother; while Dick Bodurtha, in proud defiance of the world and its conventionalities, took under her protection the one black lamb of the flock, a sorry specimen also, weak and disowned of its kind. The wretched little creatures stood but uncertainly on their long legs, which seemed in such grotesque disproportion to the rest of their bodies. They were a pitiful spectacle, which, contemplating on one occasion : —

"Do you think God made 'em, Luny?" said Dick Bodurtha, a mischievous gleam in her eyes.

Excelluna's faith was not shaken, but her look, as she stood with her finger pressed against her lips and her eyes downcast, was deeply, thoughtfully sad.

"Ever and a darlin'," said she at length; "it is true that them lambs of ourn air *not* what is generally spoke on as healthy appearin' lambs. They haven't as yit got none of them lively and friskiful ways which is generally thought on as so inter-*est*in' *in* a lamb. No, ever darlin'," said she, as the sorrowful objects of her contemplation faltered and fell weakly over, one against the other; "it is true that they air not sech as one a lookin' for mere liveliness in a lamb would be likely to pitch onto. But, ever darlin', amongst all them lambs that is caperin' around their mothers thar in the pen, amongst all them happy friskiful lambs, there is not one that has got sech a beautiful religioust look into their eyes as these 'ere lambs of ourn."

And it was true that under their hard discipline of pain and bereavement the pining little lambs had acquired something of a human piteousness of ex-pression, and looked something of a human re-sponse to the soft caresses and faithful care of their preservers. Excelluna loved Dick for that most of all. Laughing, heedless girl though she was, she never forgot to feed her lamb. It was she who woke first at midnight; for then the two left their warm beds, and guided by the dim light of their lantern, braved the night and the ghastly clatter of startled hens and horses in the barn to feed the motherless lambs.

It was all in vain. The strangely human eyes grew daily more pleading and pathetic. Excelluna's lamb died first, and that simple, compassionate heart was wrung with grief.

"You shall have mine, Luny," said Dick Bodurtha, watching her tears. "Take mine."

"Ever and a darlin'," sobbed Excelluna then; "you was good to your lamb. You was as good to your lamb as I was to mine, but you didn't feel the love like I did, elst you'd know that there couldn't never be any other lamb than 'ud be to me like that lamb, no, never!"

When Dick's lamb died, she did not cry, though she tended it faithfully to the last; and they buried them both under a tree in the orchard, where the flock grazed in the summer time. Deacon Pinchon offered them their choice again among the promising young of his flock, but they never cared for any others. If, when the sun made a golden color on the grass in the sheep orchard at evening, Excelluna, through her fur-offs, saw visions not patent to less gifted eyes, she never spoke of them; and if Dick, who loved to watch the lambs at play, thought of those quiet ones under the turf, it was only with content because their wailing, pitiful little lives were ended.

But one evening as my Dick, dabbling latest in astronomy, stood beneath the stars and discoursed to the wondering Excelluna of suns and systems numberless, over Excelluna's face, as she stood gazing upward, there suddenly came a calm and perfect illumination.

"And if that be so, ever and a darlin'," said she; "and if them be worlds sech as you speak on, with rivers and mountings and light for to lighten 'em, then, ever darlin', never doubt but *somewhere* amongst so many as could never be numbered, along them green pastur's and beside the still waters there'll be room for them poor little sorrerful lambs of ourn."

Then it was that, in an instant, there came over my Dick Bodurtha's sunny eyes a wonderful soul-shadow like an inspiration, deep, grave, beautiful; and at those words she stooped down and kissed the ancient serving-woman, at which unusual demonstration Excelluna stood motionless, beatified, beneath the stars.

CHAPTER VII.

"IT HAS COME."

"IT has come, ever and a darlin'! It has come!"
Dick Bodurtha was untying her boat down by
the river bank, when Excelluna, running breathless, confronted her with those mournfully tragic
words. That pale face, those heartbroken accents, Dick knew could mean but one thing; her
aunt had returned at length from abroad. Her
first impulse was to jump into the boat and push
swiftly down stream. Excelluna, through her
tears, did not detect the impulse — "It has come,
yis, come," she moaned; "her as has been a lookin'
of her health in forring parts."

Dick's hand was on the oar. Excelluna saw at
last.

"Ever and a darlin'," said she, growing suddenly calm, and with a numb despairing dignity in
her tone which arrested the girl's wild motion —
"many a time have I seen you rowin' of adown
that stream, with the water like glass and the sun

a shinin'; and many a time have I seen you, not fearful but more glad, with the wind a blowin' and the waves a beatin' hard. But, ever darlin', there is things as must be outgrowed. Say good-bye to the little boat now, for you must go a deeper and a further down the stream than ever the little boat will carry you."

Dick held the boat motionless. Her eyes glanced down the beckoning river, with a fine madness in them.

"Ever darlin'," Excelluna went on, with a calmness born of a heart-agony too deep — "the stream that lies before you is a long one and a sparklin', and I hear your laugh afur down and I ketch the gleamin' of your hair, and it seems ever a further and a further down, and it passes out of sight. So was you the light of poor old Luny's eyes, you was the light as her heart lived on, but now it is a passin' out of sight, and I hear the music of it afur down — for, ever darlin', the stream as I am sailin' on is a goin', not fur but swift, adark and lone to the great oshing."

The shadow, the wonderful soul-shadow, quenched the fire in Dick's eyes, and made touchingly sweet the expression of her face. She launched the boat resolutely and climbed the bank to Excelluna's side.

"I won't leave you, Luny," she said. "You shall go with me, wherever I go."

"I thank you, ever and a darlin'," said Excelluna, still in the same pathetic way; "but, no, it cannot be, never no more. For in a revelation have I seen that the streams must be divided, one a goin' a long way and a windin' and a sparklin', and the other, not fur but swift, ever darlin', alone to the great oshing."

As the two walked sadly homeward together through the familiar fields, Excelluna's speech grew more commonplace, though it was after a manner sublimely disconnected : —

"They writ as they was a comin'," said she — "so we wa'n't no more expectin' on 'em than the man in the moon — and there was yer aunt — and a nephy of Mr. Higgins — as she brought to get ye ready for school, hearin' as ye hadn't got on well with governesses, and it 'ud call for modesty and differdence — and after they come, Miss Deking went and looked in Deking's pocket — and thar was the letter, as he hadn't never thought to take it out from that time to this, — 'why, the Old

Cat!' says she, jest as slow and easy as words was ever pernounced.

"But the upshot on it is, as you air a goin' to be sent to a vary strict and religioust school, as yer aunt knows on, for to be got kinder softened ter begin with, and ter be got kinder toned down; and then you air a goin' to be sent to high-toneder schools for to be toned up. And she's brought Mr. Higginses nephy, hearin' as governesses wa'n't no use — and him bein' so bright and forring eddicated — a sayin' as 'twould call for modesty and differdence — for to get you ready to pass the examernations into that most strict and religioust school, as you must be sent to, ever darlin', for to be got toned down."

When Mrs. Bodurtha beheld her niece, she was secretly enraptured with her beauty. "This fine creature," she commented, silently; "must be duly redeemed and cultivated, and what position may she not occupy in society! Yes, she has surpassed my expectations, both in grace and beauty of person, and alas!" the lady added; "in the need which I see for corrective and softening influences." For Dick's cheek, as Mrs. Bodurtha folded the girl in her embrace, was turned to her aunt in a manner ungraciously irresponsive. The aunt forgot everything, however, in a sudden glow, not so much of affection as of enthusiasm for the future glory of her family, to be attained in the lovely person of Dick Bodurtha. "You must *learn* to love me, my child," she said, and relinquished the small sunburned hand, as she gazed down at it with a sigh.

With surprise Mrs. Bodurtha watched Dick's perfectly frank and cordial manner towards the bright youth, Scanlan Higgins. "My niece's conduct," she continued, in sarcastic musing; "is evidently not to be hampered by any blushing instincts of timidity. She essays to express her likes and dislikes absolutely without hesitation or embarrassment; a privilege which, I fear, she will be obliged to forego one of these days, when she shall have learned to assume some things, and, above all, not hold to people in that horribly long, crude way with her eyes."

The young ladies' seminary at Mount Grimrood, for which Dick was destined, would open in two weeks. Two weeks had Scanlan Higgins in which to test Dick's qualifications, and prepare her in whatever might be found wanting, necessary to her success in passing the preliminary examinations of the school.

"I shall win her confidence first," said the talented boy to Mrs. Bodurtha; "by joining her in her out-of-door sports, and conversing with her quite freely and naturally on indifferent subjects." And he devoted himself so enthusiastically to this pursuit that, led on by Dick's genius and daring, it appeared that he had well nigh forgotten at last the ostensible object of his mission to Dymsbury Park. Their voices rang merrily on the river, and the roads about Dymsbury Park resounded with the clatter of their horses' hoofs.

Mrs. Bodurtha mused grimly and in blank dismay. "I knew," said she; "from the first, that I was fated to fail wherever I touched this child's career. In placing her with these tenants of mine, I subjected her, as I supposed, to the most rigorous and uncompromising discipline. I have not yet fully realized the magnitude of my mistake, but I have seen enough to know that it has been absolute and complete. I brought Scanlan with me to prepare the girl in her studies, thinking it would, if anything, call for the exercise of maidenly modesty and reserve on her part: and it seems that

I have simply furnished the whirlwind with a play-fellow."

"Have you won my niece's confidence yet, Scanlan?" she observed with cool irony, on the sixth day, as Scanlan came in from a spirited race with Dick on horseback.

Scanlan Higgins, who was a good lad, blushed frankly: "We needn't feel any concern about her education, Mrs. Bodurtha," he said. "It surprises me. She uses magnificent language, and quotes no end of heathen poets and philosophers."

But that very same evening, as he stood in the library with Dick, he was moved carelessly to pick up a volume from a pile of old text-books on the floor, and, waving his hand in the direction of the library shelves, "Of course you know more about all this sort of thing than I do," he said: "but," he continued, laughing; "I'm afraid you have not been informed that I came here for the express purpose of finding out the vast extent of your learning, and I shall now proceed with the examination. Will you oblige me by performing this example?" And he opened an arithmetic at the last few crucial problems in fractions.

Dick glanced slightly at the problem, and then

lifted her eyes to Scanlan's face with a mocking glance, and one as bright and dauntless as it was incredulous. Somehow Scanlan understood she had not got so far as that. He was shocked and surprised, but he cast down his eyes with a gentle and apologetic intention. Dick took the book, and, turning to the familiar pages of simple addition, a mathematical height to which having attained under the tuition of the faithful Excelluna, both teacher and pupil had been compelled to pause, there revealed the traces of a painful and arduous struggle. From the labored pencil-marks on the margin of the page, Scanlan Higgins saw that, added together, —

$$\begin{array}{r} \text{``}9083 \\ 8627 \\ \hline \end{array}$$

equal . . . 1761010,"

and for a moment he was speechless.

Dick never lifted her wide, intent eyes from his face. "Is it right, Scanlan?" she said at length, in a tone so gentle and composed that the youth started violently.

"Right!" he exclaimed, forgetting the annoying problem in view of the bewitching beauty of the girl's face; "it is inimitable! It is perfect,

matchless! We will consider the examination at
once and forever closed."

Dick, though ignorant of arithmetic, was quick
at detecting the essences of things, and brave in
parrying any thrusts which might tend to her self-
mortification. She continued to hold the heated
youth for a moment in what Mrs. Bodurtha had
termed "that long crude way with her eyes," and
then coolly turned and left the room.

Dick went down to where Cadmus Pinchon
Junior, sat on the fence, in the starlight, seeking
solace from a watermelon. Cadmus Junior felt
that the air about Dymsbury Park had been growing desolate of late. He had been graduated at
the Dymsbury Academy, and was going away in a
few weeks to be apprenticed to his uncle, a wool
merchant, in Boston. Dick was going away. Dick
was occupied with her tutor. All the old associations were being broken up. There was a vague
feeling of sadness in Cadmus Junior's bosom, but
after all, his supreme sense was one of enjoyment
in the watermelon.

"I'm very sorry to think of leaving Dymsbury
Park, Caddie," said Dick, coming up in the old
homelike, confidential way.

"I'm some sorry *I'm* goin' away," said Cadmus. "But I'm goin' inter business, and I shall make lots of money. Perhaps some of these fellows that feel so big and know everything 'll be glad to be in my shoes, by and by."

Dick knew that Cadmus referred, though without the poetry of any jealous or sentimental emotion, to Scanlan Higgins. The wound caused by the noxious problem rankled in her breast. She was full of sympathy for Cadmus. "It don't make any difference what your acquirements are if you only have a manly soul, Caddie," she said.

Cadmus Junior who, had not dabbled in philosophy, could not appreciate the artistic beauty of this remark, but he felt that the sentiment was republican, and he warmed at it. Cadmus had never thought of being *spoony* on Dick. He was frequently puzzled at her, and he found her "queer," a characteristic which he regarded on the whole as exceedingly unfortunate. "I want a girl to *be* a girl," he confided once to a boy companion; "and wear white aprons, and squeal at toads and things, and not be too smarty. But then," he admitted; "if you're in for a real good time, there ain't a boy in Dymsbury that's got so much gumption as Towhead." Now, as he sat contemplating her for a moment quite indifferently beneath the stars, it occurred to him that her hair had a wonderful gleam in it,— and her eyes, submitted to this close and unusual scrutiny, he found rather bewildering, but a glance at the heavens over the disc of his watermelon enlighted and reassured him.

" Say, Towhead," said he, in a profoundly prosaic tone, touched with a slight accent of surprise; "your eyes have got something just like stars in 'em, they have, honest ! "

Dick smiled. " I shall always remember you, Caddie," said she; " and the pleasant times we have had together."

" And me you," said Cadmus, definitively, as not wishing to approach any nearer the verge of conventional sentiment.

The next day, and for several days, Dick, with sincere tenderness at the thought of parting, courted the society of Cadmus Junior and the little Pinchons.

" I should infer that my niece and her felicitously chosen tutor are what is termed in childish parlance 'mad,' " Mrs. Bodurtha reflected; " and it is an intense relief to me.   I only hope they may remain so until I get the girl safely off to school."

But on the morning of the last whole day at Dymsbury Park, Dick and Scanlan made up; and Dick's relentings were always of a dangerous and irresistible nature to the party received back again into favor.   After that it came about quite naturally, as they rocked idly in the boat together, that the gentle boy expressed a hope that Dick at some future day might be the guiding star and companion of his life.   The untamed lass replied, with a majestic seriousness and composure of manner which would still more have surprised the distracted Mrs. Bodurtha, that she had formed plans for the future amelioration of the race which must forever debar her from participating in domestic joys.   At the same time, Dick, having admitted to the eccentric range of her acquirements a flavor of very ancient, very daring and inconsequent romance, suggested that they should " elope " together that night, just for the rare fun of the thing ; to return, of course, in a day or two, but it would be very delightful and exciting.

Scanlan was grieved and disheartened at Dick's childishness, but he dreamed too long in her unfathomable eyes, and he did not refuse to elope with her. Dick arranged all the preliminaries of the escapade by the light of a true poetic imagination.

At the hour before midnight the stamping of horses' hoofs was heard underneath her window, and Scanlan gave a low whistle. Dick, already arrayed, hastened to the window.

" Art ready, beloved lady?" Scanlan repeated, in a tone of much seriousness and sweetness.

"Ready, dear knight," Dick answered, with a smothered giggle ; for the horses under the window, though well adapted to purposes of elopement, or to any other requiring speed and endurance, did have a comical and unromantic look.

Dick descended on the rope-ladder previously prepared, and the two mounted and were off. After a hard gallop of some miles, even Dick's imagination could find no stimulus in listening for the swift rush of pursuing feet. The mist came up chill from the river; and it was not one o'clock when the wanderers returned. But the Deacon Cadmus Pinchon family had been aroused, and Mrs. Bodurtha's handsome face was pale and her lips compressed. Yet so relieved was she at the unexpected return of the miscreants, which she considered as an act of repentance on their part, that she merely sent them, with severe dignity, to their beds. "I shall sleep no more to-night," said she; "and, thank Heaven! to-morrow this will be ended."

Dick lay in the dark, with her lips curled and a wide, defiant smile in her eyes, when she was aware that a gentle presence had come in and seated itself at the foot of her bed :—

"Ever and a darlin'," said the voice — and it was the voice of one who had struggled and who stood solemnly on a clear height — "I've been a thinkin' and a thinkin'. Weary has been my thoughts and sorrerful my heart, but now there's a more of a stillness — there's a more of a stillness, ever darlin', along the sorrerful road. I've been a thinkin' as maybe it's best for you, fur, fur best for you, for to go and be toned down. Not but what I know as it's a breakin' up a good many of your plans, and how you was a studyin' natur', and, when you get through a havin' fun, you was goin' to be a great preacher for to draw 'em all; and, ever darlin', there was no plan as ever you formed but poor old Luny's heart was with you, a waitin' for to see that day.

"But, ever darlin'," continued the old serving-woman, with sad and grand simplicity; "in this 'ere world of ourn, so weary and so pitiful, and all a strugglin' for to know their own and hold it fast, and oft beat out and disapp'inted, there ain't but one plan a runnin' through it all, not but jest one plan —

"And so I've been a thinkin', and I've thunk it all out ; it's like as ef you should feel somebody drawin' of you along a dark, onsarting road, and you a thinkin' as there might be easier roads, and heart-broke, fearin' as you've lost the way ; but fear not, ever darlin', for in a revelation have I seen as that 'ar road that looked so dark and wanderin', that 'ar only sorrerful road, is a plain road and a straight, and is a leadin' of us home.

"And, ever darlin, there's an angeling mother's hand a leadin' you along that road —— "

"Don't!" cried Dick, with a little restless scream of pain.

"There's an angeling mother's hand, and she whispers to you to be gentle and obejent and to put off wildness :" — and the old serving-woman continued talking with supreme fervor, sitting meekly at the foot of the bed. But when she rose to go, she touched the cheek of the girl, who had fallen asleep then, and found that it was cold and wet with tears.

"Poor beautiful lamb!" Excelluna sobbed. "She's nothin' but a child, and she only loves a little. But she was the light of poor old Luny's eyes, she was the light as her heart lived on. It has come! It has come!"—Excelluna ceased suddenly to weep, lifting an awestruck face— "There's a more of a stillness," she said; "along the sorrerful road."

CHAPTER VIII.

A SUBJECT FOR MOUNT GRIMROOD FEMALE SEMINARY.

THE elder Mr. Higgins came to escort my young lady to Mount Grimrood, and Mrs. Bodurtha went back in cold triumph with Scanlan to New York.

It was unfortunate that Dick should have had a natural antipathy for both her aunt and her guardian. She did not like the tone in which Mr. Higgins now occasionally addressed her as "Miss Bodurtha," any better than that in which he had formerly been wont to call her " my cha-ah-ming child." But he took her purse—Dick affected in those days a very manly and capacious pocket-book, it had ten alcoves, she tells me, and a leathern strap — and filled it with crisp new bank notes.

" You must never allow yourself to get out of money, my dear," he said. " Write directly to me. And, by the way, you musn't let them make you *too* meek at this place you are going to. We can't have the spirits crushed out of our cha-ha-ming little girl. To tell you the truth," continued this wise guardian to his ward; "I didn't exactly like the idea of sending you to Mount Grimrood. But your aunt seemed to think it was a desperate case and called for desperate expedients. And I dare say you'll be vastly edified; but you must hold your own, you musn't let them run over you, you know."

Gratified at the plethoric state of her pocket-book, Dick nodded graciously at the words her guardian whispered in her ear; but after all there was little danger that Dick's conduct would be guided by any extraneous advice.

At Cramingham, where they waited for the train to Johnston's Ferry, Mr. Higgins received a telegram of great business importance, recalling him immediately to New York; and Dick, with infinite satisfaction, contemplated pursuing the brief remainder of her journey alone.

Dick, introduced to the travelling community, observed a general tendency on the part of people to stare. This struck her as perfectly natural. She did not know that she made a quaint, attractive picture in the workaday world, but she thought people very interesting and frequently comical, and returned the glances cast in her direction with a frank and cordial scrutiny which concealed neither its own delectation nor occasional surprise. That gaze, too childlike and sincere to be insolent, yet had a cool, bright courage in it which defied criticism, and threw off lightly any insinuating glances of evil.

Arrived at Johnston's Ferry, Dick found her way to the big boat and the river; the river — it was wider, deeper than the stream at Dymsbury, and it was sullen gray with the approach of evening. It seemed as though Dick must feel everything through external nature. It was the river that brought that aching sense to her heart; the river, reminding her of that brighter stream far away, winding, willow-fringed; that desolate stream, now, with its empty boat, rocking, waiting forevermore, idle under the willows.

The ferry-boat was full of passengers. Dick had not noticed. She stood looking out on the water with one hand thrust lightly in the breast of her jacket. She wore a velvet jacket of hunter's-green and a short skirt, with wide collar and cuffs, already considerably soiled from her journey, and a plumed hat set jauntily on her head. Her eyes looked dreamy and sad; her lips were parted slightly, in this abstracted mood; and the wind blew her light hair about her face.

In spite of its careless, unworn beauty, there was a look on the young face that haunted one. It was sadder than home-sickness, for it had not that tenderness. It seemed vainly trying to comprehend its own want; it was such a vague, tearless wonder and yearning.

Turning at last to contemplate her fellow-passengers, Dick was astonished to find that the boat was filled, save for the old ferryman, with females exclusively. Some of them were young and pretty, but they were all primly dressed, and most of them struck Dick, at that gloomy hour, as being of an uncommonly severe type. There was one woman especially, with a marble face and great relentless black eyes, who looked at Dick. Dick shivered. For the first time in her life an expression almost of fear crossed her face. If she had been in the least of a practical turn of mind, she would have divined that these were the pupils and teachers of Mount Grimrood Seminary on their way thither — but, poor Dick, she had never been put to the trouble of connecting causes and effects in her mind. She took in the scene solely in its immediately apparent and poetic sense; and, to her, this galaxy of black-stoled and unmated women, crossing a shadowy stream at the twilight hour, appeared incomprehensible and terribly picturesque.

She crossed over to where the old ferryman, silently, but with a red and jovial face, was tugging the boat along by the wire cables stretched across the river. There was something pathetic in the manner in which Dick drew this man into a conversation on the technology of boats, and he appreciated it.

"Here's a mighty han'som and a wild one," he said to himself; "sent to be tamed down a bit, I bet ye! wall, they get a hold of 'em once in a while. But she don't know how she's a makin' their eyes stick out o' their heads by comin' over here and 'sociatin' with me so nateral, now does she?" So he chuckled, and entertained Dick with stories, and Dick recounted some thrilling adventures of her own. She was rapidly recovering her spirits. She sat, in a precarious position, on the edge of the boat, and traced invisible hieroglyphics with a lead-pencil on the toe of her slightly elevated boot.   She spoke in a tone that, without containing any loudly aggressive quality, was yet distinctly audible throughout the length and breadth of the boat : —

"Why don't there any men or boys go over on this boat ? " she said.

Poor Dick ! she little knew what she had done. And even if she had been informed that the person who stood at her very elbow, the woman with the marble face and relentless eyes, was Miss Calvin, the assistant principal of Mount Grimrood Seminary, how could she have calculated the appalling effect of her words upon the virgin souls of the teachers and pupils of that august institution ? Even the old ferryman stood for a moment aghast : —

"Here *is* a fresh one and a gay one," he reflected, and he kindly tried to catch Dick's eye, in intimation of danger, and coughed suggestively.   But Dick did not notice.

"Why don't there any men or boys go over in this boat ? " she repeated, in the same clear tone.

"Why, miss," stammered the old ferryman;

"what would the men and boys be going to Mount Grimrood for, miss ? "

" Why," said Dick, her eyes wandering dreamily towards the mountains on the opposite shore ; " it isn't the end of the world over there, is it ? "

" No," responded the old ferryman, desperately ; " it ain't, but it's the end of the men-folks."

Dick sighed, and her sigh was distinctly regretful and as unembarrassed as her speech.

Presently, "It's a pretty prim place over there, I expect," she remarked, with singular fatuity.   Her eyes, fixed full on the ferryman's face, had a cheerful smile of inquiry in them, which, under more favorable circumstances, would doubtless have elicited from him a thoroughly facetious and exhaustive response.   As it was, he could only mutter to himself, as he bent to his work : —

" She's in for it now.   She may as well die for a a whole sheep as a lamb."

Dick thought her humble companion was growing inattentive.   She proceeded to crush him with a few well-chosen words from her vocabulary : "I hope there won't be too much stiffness in the atmosphere, over there," she said, giving her undivided attention to the scenery ; "I'm very susceptible to any stiffness in the atmosphere."

At that moment, on Dick's little, warm, brown hand, there fell an icy touch : " Young woman," said the voice of Miss Calvin, in her ear ; "your position is most indecorous, and you are in imminent danger of falling into the water."

" Oh," said Dick, pleasantly enough, but with a startled, curious look in her eyes as she lifted them to that impassive face ; " I can swim — like anything ! Can you swim ? "

Slowly and unsmilingly Miss Calvin shook her awful head.

" Everybody ought to know how," said Dick. She had a little struggle with herself, for the woman who stood over her was very repellant to her, and then continued magnanimously ; " I'm going to be at Mount Grimrood, and if you live anywhere about here, I'll show you, if you like."

" Child," responded Miss Calvin, "*I* am going to be at Mount Grimrood. The persons standing about us in the boat, who have witnessed your singular and unseemly conduct, are going to be at Mount Grimrood. Lest your thoughtlessness should lead you into further indiscretions, it is well that I should inform you that we are all teachers and pupils of Mount Grimrood Seminary."

Dick grew more and more puzzled: "Now she's mad," she mused sagely; "because I said I thought they might be a prim set over there." But Dick attempted no apology. She armed herself straightway for a conflict, after the artless fashion peculiar to Dymsbury Park. With a sweet flame in her cheeks, she set her white teeth in Miss Calvin's very face, and her brown eyes flashed a cheerful defiance.

"Child," said Miss Calvin; "I shall not reason with you further *here:*" and she withdrew her icy hand.

The old ferryman looked as though he would have jumped into the river. His cheeks had a dangerously red and explosive aspect. "Sure enough," he muttered under his breath; "here *is* a high one and a mad lark, and when the old She fretted her, gad, if she didn't turn and show fight! But she dies for a whole sheep, mind ye. She don't die for no lambs!" And it was almost with awe and admiration that he watched Dick, when, the boat being landed, she smiled condescendingly down on him from her perch by the side of the stage-driver. "She dies for a whole sheep, mind ye," he repeated; "she don't die for no lambs."

The stage stopped at the side entrance of a large brick pile, and Dick passed into Mount Grimrood Seminary. The inexorable Miss Calvin was at her elbow. She guided my lass by her chill touch into a room styled the "South Wing Receptory," where there sat a dignified conclave of teachers, and, in their midst, Miss Milton, the principal of Mount Grimrood. Miss Milton was tall, of a gaunt, loose frame; but Dick thought her face was very strong and fine. Her spare cheeks were flushed as if with weariness or excitement. Her throat filled often, so that her speech, though of a tender and impressive tone, was painfully labored. Still guided by Miss Calvin's hand, Dick felt herself impelled into the immediate presence of this august individual. Miss Calvin then stooped down and whispered in Miss Milton's ear. Miss Milton looked at Dick and smiled kindly, and, taking the girl's hand, drew her gently to one side, retaining her while the ordinary business of the hour went on. One by one those who had crossed the ferry with

Dick and arrived at Mount Grimrood in the same line of stages, were welcomed and dismissed by Miss Milton, who never let go her firm hold of the girl's hand. Dick began to feel the position as a tiresome and disagreeably conspicuous one. The touch that had at first seemed to her so kind, she now began to resent as hateful and cruel. Inclined by nature to stand up valiantly for her own rights, her acquaintance with the young Pinchons and the lads at Dymsbury had not fostered in her any shrinking timidity of disposition. Careless dreamer as she was, she had entertained no hostile emotions on entering Mount Grimrood. She chose to be conciliatory, but, if they put her to it, she would not hesitate to bay them all. " I'll be even with you some time," she whispered through her gleaming teeth to a shrinking junior, who, in passing, had stared at her too inquisitively. " Hallo, old Flyaway!" she murmured to a female in an escalloped white basque and with floating ringlets, who had not concealed a shade of disapproval on her face as she looked at Dick. Dick supposed that this was a senior pupil, but it was, in fact, one of the younger teachers at Mount Grimrood, and her name was Miss Bean.

The last pupil had been dismissed. The teachers also rose and left the room, and then Miss Milton drew Dick to a large ottoman at her feet, and gently released her hand.

"I kept you waiting — my child " — she said, in her kind, labored speech; " because — as we have received you to the Seminary — under rather peculiar circumstances — having in fact been definitely informed — by your aunt — as to your requirements and past life — I thought it better — that I should see you alone. Will you tell me — your name ? "

" Dick," replied my lass, in a tone which it was possible to deplore as marked by too clear an emphasis.

"Your name," said the principal of Mount Grimrood; " I have been informed —on no less authority — than your own aunt — is Lucy — Lucy Bodurtha — and thus you will be known — during your stay — at this institution."

Dick, at white heat, smiled hopefully to herself, and said nothing.

" And how old are you, my child ? " Miss Milton continued.

" Sixteen," Dick replied.

"Sixteen!" exclaimed Miss Milton, with prudently affected surprise. "Sixteen! and so tall!—and still with a childish nickname! and all this beautiful hair hanging unconfined down your back! and your dress scarcely reaching to the tops of your boots!"

Still Dick smiled hopefully to herself and said nothing. Miss Milton allowed her hand to wander caressingly through the light tresses of Dick's unconfined hair; and, as she did so, the dignity of her office and the cares of her devoted life slipped for a moment from her mind, and her flushed face grew restful and dreamy.

"And do you know"—she continued, recovering herself—"what was your object in coming—or your friend's object—in sending you—to Mount Grimrood?"

Dick felt that it was too bad, her aunt having evidently disclosed all, and more than the truth, that she should be compelled to repeat the obnoxious phrase. However ——

"I came," she answered, resolutely; "*to be toned down.*"

An incredulous, almost an appreciative smile passed over Miss Milton's face, Dick's manner was calculated to awaken such lively hopes in the breast of those who should be called to perform that office for her, and there was only such a mad seriousness in the girl's face.

"You came," Miss Milton answered, gently; "to perform — a faithful course of study — and to find your highest pleasure — in conforming to those regulations — which it is necessary for us to make — and to enforce. The examinations for admission begin to-morrow. You have yet some time — before the retiring bell — to spend in study. I have considered it best — that you should room for the present with two seniors — they are estimable young ladies — and I hope — you will grow warmly — attached to them. Their names — are Miss F. Armenia Stetson — and Miss B. Arabella Bell."

"I don't think I should like rooming with two of those seniors," said Dick, firmly, though with great simplicity of manner. "I don't think it would be very comfortable. Somehow, I don't believe I should sleep well."

Miss Milton could only look her questioning surprise.

"Because," continued Dick; "they're too bony and studious."

"My child," Miss Milton interrupted quickly, "let us pray."

As Miss Milton knelt on the floor at Dick's side the passion in the girl's heart changed slowly to wonder, but at the sound of that tired, earnest voice in supplication she was touched.

"I enjoyed your prayer very much," she said, as they passed out of the room together — for Miss Milton herself had undertaken to show Dick to her room. Miss Milton turned and looked sharply at Dick, but found no cause for suspicion in that lovely, ingenuous face. Miss Calvin had been wiser. She had taken firm ground at the beginning that Dick's nature was hopelessly depraved, and had arranged her forces for a distinct conflict. But Miss Milton, unconsciously to herself, had already begun to make a study of the lass; and when one would make a study of my Dick — well, I know that that proved sometimes dangerous.

Miss Milton introduced Dick to her room-mates, Miss F. Armenia Stetson and Miss B. Arabella Bell, and withdrew. Those young ladies were studying when Dick entered the room. They rose gravely and saluted her, and then seated themselves immediately at their books again. Dick contemplated them for some moments in silence; they had dark ringlets, a freak of nature with which she had already become familiar at Mount Grimrood, and pale and composed faces. Besides the shade on the lamp, they wore shades that covered the lower part of their foreheads and jutted out over their eyes and were tied behind their ears. Dick had seen the same sort of arrangement in connection with unruly animals, and she was well acquainted with the use of the "blinders" for horses; but of overtaxed nerves and the habits of those who study by lamplight she knew nothing.

"I wonder," she meditated, "whether those two jump fences or shy."

The silence grew very tedious. Dick finally concluded to address one of them, but she was a little perplexed how she should call her name.

"B. ?" said she, good-naturedly, and received no answer. "B. Arabella ?" said Dick.

B. Arabella looked up and placed a finger admonishingly on her lips. A moment afterwards the sound of a bell was heard in the hall. "I did not speak to you before," she then said, "because we are not permitted to speak in study hours. We have now a recess of a few moments." She smiled at Dick feebly and inquiringly.

Dick returned the smile. "I've just come," she said; "and it doesn't seem to be a very lively place, and I thought you might entertain me a little."

Miss F. Armenia Stetson and Miss B. Arabella Bell looked at each other. They were not likely to be deluded into making a study of Dick ; and, as they still sat looking at each other, the bell rang again.

Dick wandered out into the halls. Occasionally some one passed through, and that afforded a little diversion. But a teacher found her thus employed and, "Do you not know," she said; "that it is against our rules to delay unnecessarily in the halls ? "

So Dick found some stairs and sat disconsolately down on them. She had not been there long, when she heard a cheerful rushing sound over her head ; and, ere she had time to turn, a girl of about her own age, with brown hair cut short like a boy's, and dancing blue eyes, swept by her at a wild rate down the banisters. An angel from heaven could not have brought such a sudden thrill of joy to Dick's heart. As the blue-eyed girl dismounted and turned to ascend the stairs again, it was tacitly understood by both that Dick should join her, and by the time they had taken several bouts on the banisters together they were as well acquainted as though they had known each other from child-hood.

The merry blue-eyed girl confided to Dick that her father and mother were missionaries, that she had been born on a heathen island; and that her name was Hawaii; that her parents had given her in trust to Mount Grimrood Seminary, and that, when she got old enough, she was "dedicated to go and be a missionary, too." This last she shouted at Dick in a shrill tone, while they were going so rapidly down the banisters that Hawaii's short hair stood out perpendicularly from her head, and Dick's golden mane floated behind her like a cloud.

Dick's life and prospects seemed very tame to her in comparison with Hawaii's. She told her friend briefly that her name was Dick Bodurtha, that she was an orphan and "very wicked," — a fact which she had discovered since coming to

Mount Grimrood and upon which she now dwelt with peculiar pride — and had been sent to Mount Grimrood to be *toned down.*

"Have they put you in with two seniors?" asked Hawaii.

"Yes," said Dick.

"They have me, too," said Hawaii, with cheerful pride; "they always put the bad ones in with two seniors."

They were making a particularly illustrious descent when seized upon at the foot of the stairs by no less a personage than Miss Calvin herself; who rebuked them icily and sent them to their rooms. But Dick had not been confined many moments in her prison-house with F. Armenia Stetson and B. Arabella Bell, before she heard a slight enticing cough in the hall. She crept out. Oh, joy! It was Hawaii. "Get your night-gown, Dick," she whispered; "I've found a nice airy sleeping-room that we can have all to ourselves."

Dick went cautiously back for her night-gown, and followed Hawaii through the halls and up the stairs, up, up, ever higher up; still there was another flight, winding and steep and dark; and then, in the cupola of Mount Grimrood Seminary at last, the air blew fresh and strong on their cheeks, and the stars shone down on them. There Hawaii had arranged a couch with blankets and pillows which she had confiscated from the regions below. Hawaii took off her cotton-gown and Dick disrobed herself of her velvet, and the two friends lay down in their white dresses. And Hawaii slept. And Dick wandered lightly back to Dymsbury Park, where the starlight shone on the familiar places, and the great elms outside sighed and waved, and Excelluna, through her fur-offs, talked with God; and then Dick slept.

Below rang the hour-bell before retiring, the half-hour bell, the quarter-of-an-hour bell, the five-minutes bell, the solemn retiring-bell — and still Dick and Hawaii slept.

Then F. Armenia Stetson and B. Arabella Bell, with Hawaii's room-mates, alarmed the teachers, and Mount Grimrood Seminary was aroused, and search for Dick and Hawaii was made in every quarter of that great building and throughout the adjacent grounds.

It was Miss Milton herself who first ascended the steep stairs that led to that utmost height;

but before the others came up, and before she should find it necessary sternly to arouse those placid sleepers, she stooped down with an almost impulsive gesture and stroked Dick's quiet face.

CHAPTER IX.

"PUT ME IN WITH THE GOATS."

DICK'S descent from the cupola had been a hazy one, and she was considerably surprised the next morning, when awakened by B. Arabella Bell. B. Arabella had arisen and dressed by lamplight, and her book lay open on the table. "Would you not like," she said to Dick; "to get into the habit, which Miss Stetson and I have formed, of taking our devotional half-hour before breakfast ? "

"Taking a what ? " said Dick, only half awakened, her eyes opening vague with wonder.

" It is one of the excellent rules of the institution," said B. Arabella ; " that those who enjoy its advantages shall take a devotional half-hour in perfect solitude twice every day. If you make haste to dress, you will have just time to complete your morning half-hour ere breakfast. Miss Stetson has gone out to find a solitary place in which to take hers; I will take mine here, and the closet," said B. Arabella, pointing to a gloomy aperture at one end of the room; "is at your disposal."

The prospect of fleeing from the presence of B. Arabella Bell, even into the darkness, was an agreeable one. Dick hastily dressed herself as well as she might without Excelluna's aid, and repaired to the closet. A chink at the bottom of the door let in a faint ray of light; Dick discovered a wooden stool and sat down upon it — sleepy, homeless, motherless girl, her head drooped on her shoulder, she said over the little prayer with which Excelluna had taught her to begin the day at Dymsbury Park, and tried to realize the general doleful horrors of her situation at Mount Grimrood Seminary; but sleep soon came to her relief. Meantime, rang all the little bells again; and at the sound of the breakfast bell, B. Arabella rose from her devotions, and joined F. Armenia Stetson and the throng in the halls, but Dick slept on, in glad unconsciousness of closet or darkness, or the fact that to be tardy at breakfast at Mount Grimrood Seminary was a strange and well-nigh inexcusable offence.

It was Hawaii, concealed under a table near the

wide entrance of the dining-hall — Hawaii, peering out, bright-eyed and alert as some ground-burrowing animal, her short hair all erect with a morning crispness — who noted Dick's absence and rushed forth to find her. But when Hawaii, laughing, dragged Dick out of the closet, Dick woke to the situation with solemn wrath and defiance. "We lived with God all the time at Dymsbury Park," she said, as they walked through the hall together; and Hawaii ceased laughing, and wondered, looking into Dick's eyes, for they were not like any ordinary eyes that she had seen, but they reminded her directly of sun, and deep, and sudden storm. "We lived with God all the time at Dymsbury Park. I sha'n't take any more of their half-hours," said Dick, gravely and savagely.

When they reached the dining-hall their spirits rose. There were sixteen tables spread, twenty girls or more at each table, with teachers presiding; in their midst, Dick discovered Miss Milton's tall form. It was just at the solemn moment, when, standing after silent grace, the company waited for Miss Milton to take the initiative by drawing forth her chair and seating herself, that my Dick and Hawaii appeared, smiling, on the scene. It occurred to those two immortal spirits that, at so many tables, very likely there might be a choice of viands ; and they proceeded, by an agreement affecting their mutual advantage, to make an impartial *détour* of the dining-room and to give immediate oral testimony as to their discoveries.

“ Hash, here !” cried Hawaii, beginning her cheerful tour of inspection.

“ Hash, here !” Dick responded clearly from another direction.

“ Hash, here !” re-echoed Hawaii, proceeding still farther down the line, but with an undeniable shade of disappointment growing in her tone.

“ Hash —,” Dick began again, but the obnoxious phrase died incomplete on her lips. Miss Calvin’s icy touch chilled and drew her to the table where she herself presided, and where also sat Miss Bean. Miss Bean, whom Dick had casually addressed the night before as “ Old Fly-away,” gravely poised her ringleted head and gazed at my lass with deep pity and distrust.

Hawaii’s career had also been arrested at another point. Dick’s heart yearned for her lively companion, yet she allowed neither obloquy nor sentiment to interfere with the dictates of her fresh young appetite. She ignored the hash with an expression of innocent disfavor, but partook plentifully of bread and prunes, and passed her small tumbler many times for water. That she was regarded, in some sort, as a criminal waiting for execution, she could not but perceive; yet were her clear and challenging eyes strangely devoid of fear. It was the sublime sentiment imbibed at Dymsbury Park, in every emergency to "die game."

After breakfast, Dick was led away by Miss Bean and subjected to an inquisition of half an hour, which she bore coolly and with an aptness and fortitude of rejoinder already augmented by her brief sojourn at Mount Grimrood. Released by Miss Bean, she learned that Miss Milton wished to see her immediately in her private apartment. But Dick had discovered the human chord hidden away in Miss Milton's awful bosom, and the child struck at it with artless confidence and abandon. Strangely fascinating grew the study of this neglected nature to Miss Milton, but she conscientiously repressed the yearning impulse as a foe to her august duty. Long and severely she lectured Dick, until the bell rang for united devotions in the seminary hall.

Then was it indeed a solemn sight, when the three hundred and sixty pupils of the Mount Grimrood female seminary were seated silently in the seminary hall, and on the platform above, the forty teachers — Miss Milton in their midst; at her right, Miss Calvin; at her left, another senior potentate; and so on, down the scale of importance, to Miss Bean at one extreme, and a certain Miss Ratting at the other. It was a solemn spectacle.

Then rose Miss Milton, and slightly bowed her awe-inspiring frame, and murmured, with a ghastly attempt at cheer, which checked for an instant the free blood in Dick's veins; "Good morning, young ladies."

And all the young ladies rose and bowed themselves and sat down again, and again was silence.

Miss Milton then read, as was the custom at the beginning of each school year, the peculiar rules to be observed at Mount Grimrood Seminary.

And all the pupils listened and wrote. And having covered several sheets of foolscap with her black and daring chirography, it occurred to wicked Dick that matters might have been greatly facilitated by mentioning the one or two things that it

was proper to do at Mount Grimrood, such as
eating principally with one's fork, and drawing, in a
repressed and decorous fashion, the necessary
breath of life.

After this exercise, came the ordinary morning
devotions, touching and appropriate ; and the singing, very sweet, except for a certain narrow-chested,
high-pitched quality of tone.   Then it was evident
that something of unusual importance was about to
occur.   Miss Milton, from her throne, cleared her
throat several times, ere she spoke in grave and
measured accents : —

"It is our custom — young ladies — for many
eminent reasons — and especially — that we may
the more intelligently exert that religious influence — which it is the peculiar design — of our
beloved institution to exert — it is our custom —
to ascertain — the exact religious status — of each
of our pupils.   Will those — who are members —
of our Christian churches — now rise?"

At this Dick observed that a large portion of
the assembly rose.   Their names were called and
duly taken down by a scribe upon the throne.

Miss Milton again cleared her throat, and again
spoke, now with a singularly affecting earnestness:

"Will those — who — though they have been hindered — by some untoward circumstance — from uniting — with our beloved churches — who yet — mayhap — love God — who —" Miss Milton paused a moment as her throat filled, and then added — "now rise?"

Among the number who rose at this summons, quite happily and unconsciously rose my Dick — my Dick, for whom it was so easy to fall a dreaming. And the dream was in her eyes — God, who filled all things at Dymsbury Park, from mighty day-beam to plaintive bird-note; ay, and with whom dear old Excelluna talked, and from whom she had had so many, many revelations. Dreaming, it escaped Dick that she was now so wicked. Quite happily and unconciously she rose, for surely she loved God!

The names of these also were reported, and duly taken down, with modified approval by the scribe upon the throne.

Still were there some who had not risen at all. And as the names of those were written, be it said, with all reverence for the undoubted sincerity of the act, that some of those upon the throne wept.

A deeper solemnity settled upon the scene. The pupils seated themselves once more ; and in a tone still more measured and portentous, Miss Milton read, from the twenty-fifth chapter of Matthew, the awful allegory of the final tragic separation of the sheep from the goats. Slowly and impressively she read ; and at the close, " This hour also," she said ; "is typical — of that final — sad event. Even now — young ladies," — and a heavy atmosphere as of death settled over the assembly — " though — in this world — there is hope of reclamation — even now — young ladies — in some sense — as the shepherd divideth his sheep from the goats —" But suddenly, as she listened, my Dick awoke from her dreaming. This was not the God of Dymsbury Park, whose sun shone on waste and pool, whose free wind blew over all ; the vile was ever being purified ; the base climbed ever towards the light. Excelluna had not told her of this ; of difference, and election, and separation ; of endless pain and loss ; it was not in all her simple grand theology — but ever to redeem the lost, and ever hotly to defend the weak. It was the black lamb Dick had chosen. And now, as Miss Milton paused, suddenly there rose up, in the midst of the three hundred and sixty pupils, and before the forty teachers, a form of desperate insulted fire. Dick's great eyes blazed; her lips half curled with contempt, half quivered with anger. In the midst of the three hundred and sixty pupils, and before the forty teachers, a voice rang out, terribly distinct and clear in its young indignation, as Dick beckoned to the scribe upon the throne. "You may take my name off of that other sheet!" she said. "You may put me in with the goats!"

"You may put me in with the goats!"—the words resounded through the seminary hall, and the heavy atmosphere closed in upon them, heavier than before. There followed a moment, two moments, of perfect silence. Miss Milton then made a breathless sign of dismissal, and the assembly dispersed.

As, with Miss Bean and Miss Calvin following in the distance, Dick wended her way with the throng out of the seminary hall, still upborne on that towering wave of indignation, she met every cold or inquisitive or highly compassionate glance with equal defiance and scorn. Yet was the girl's heart breaking within. The memory of that dark scene, of that new and horrible revelation, lay like a pall upon her, blotting out for the instant all her fair world, changing her beautiful God to a grotesque designer of blind, insatiable wrath. Ah, where was the light that shone at Dymsbury Park; the boundless heaven and hope! Excelluna! Excelluna! Dick could have thrown herself down and wept passionately. But these who stared at her so, they should not see her bleed. She set her teeth against the rising sob. The sweet lips whitened.

So, as she passed into the outer hall, wild, reckless, inwardly sobbing, a tender, magnificent presence suddenly confronted her — a form as tall, as stately, as ample of bosom as were the other occupants of Mount Grimrood pinched and spare. Dick heard the soft rustle of silk, caught the strange gleam of precious stones, then a pair of strong, white arms enfolded her; a breath, sweet as Araby, blew on her face; a womanly, loving heart throbbed against hers, and warm kisses fell on her lips. "Run up to my room," whispered the enchanting voice; "forty-six, that is. Bean and Calvin and Ratting are all on the scent. Run, child! I shall be there in a moment."

That breath of sweet perfume, that loving

heart-throb, gave swift impulse to Dick's feet. Alone in " forty-six," whose four walls had caught something of the rich and sumptuous atmosphere of their owner, Dick waited for the beautiful, strange unknown. When the unknown entered she was fanning herself. She sat down on a sofa —it was the only sofa Dick had seen at Mount Grimrood — and drew Dick to her side. " There's no air here," she gasped, good-naturedly, as she swung her fan. " There's none to be had, though I keep my windows open day and night. They've frightened it all off within the radius of a mile at least, and they subsist on some less general and vulgar essence." But through the unknown's laughing voice, and through her resplendent attire, shone such a wholesome, bounteous, sympathetic nature, and her smiling eyes met Dick's so tenderly, that, in the one brief moment, it seemed to my lass as though the story of her sorrow had been already told and she been healed with a boundless radiance.

" Talk to me," she said, nursing one knee with all the happiness in the world. " I love you !" said she, fixing her eyes on the unknown's face with boyish, though unblushing ardor,

The smile in the unknown's eyes deepened. "In the first place, then, my beautiful child," said she; "as I am twenty-two years old and you are some years younger, I will take the liberty to suggest that there is a tolerably large rent in the skirt of your dress" — Dick thought with guilty joy of last night's ride on the banisters — "and as your weather-stained though graceful fingers proclaim great unfamiliarity with the needle, I shall be delighted to mend it for you. Meantime you may fan me.

"My name is Dakotah West. Papa's name is West. He made his fortune and lives in the West. I was born in Dakotah, and they named me Dakotah West. Quite a vasty and salubrious name, isn't it? But I was a very vigorous infant, and I have always been able to carry it off well, until now, since I came East to be cultured, and have found such a thin supply of air. Papa has no end of money, and he wanted me to be cultured, but it would break his heart if he knew how I had been scrimped for air.

"I have sojourned at various wise institutions, my dear, picking up a crumb here and there, like a belated bird in a snow-storm, and many means have been faithfully exerted in my behalf. But it is all the same. When anything strikes me as funny, I am still seized with an irresistible inclination to laugh; when anything strikes me as tearful, I weep; what I think, if I say anything, I am moved on every occasion to say; and in moments of sudden surprise or calamity, I shall probably never quite recover from a habit of giving vent to the vulgar exclamation of 'Jemimy.' No, my dear, I have a simple, kind, well-meaning nature, but I am quite convinced that I shall never be cultured."

At the delicious laughter of Dakotah's tone, Dick's head gave a delighted little bounce against that yielding shoulder.

"Always study Botany, my dear," continued Dakotah West. "Under the pretence of dissecting nature, you will get excuse for many a long ramble. I assure you, I do not know the calyx from the petal. I never yet picked an innocent flower to pieces for the mere purpose of classifying it, and, please God, I never shall. But I am a wild, ardent, and devoted student of Botany, and always take it up as a specialty when it happens not to be included in the year or in the course.

"In spite of all, I cannot but see that I am re-garded, in the beginning, even by these harpies, with a sort of favor. There is a solidity in my presence which recommends me, though my flesh and good-nature must ultimately relegate me to the society of the uncultured, and even of the unre-newed; but you, my child, you are a sylph. You mount, you fly, you disappear, you descend again. Your hair is an angel's dream. Your eyes, when a certain peculiar gleam overtakes them, I can only describe as 'deeply, darkly, beautifully' mischiev-ous. They do not in the least understand you. They will try to compose your limbs with Algebra and tame you with dialectics and frighten you with hell-fire. But there is a simple something," said Dakotah, with gentle seriousness; "that alone moves the world — to wit, namely, *love*. Be as quiet as you can, my child. When a heaven-born idea strikes you, occasionally reserve it. Yet I greatly fear me that the walls of Mount Grimrood will not contain you long."

Dick's head gave another bounce against Da-kotah's shoulder, and rested there. Dakotah put down her needle and drew Dick up in her arms, and stroked her golden mane. "You don't mind

my calling you Towhead?" she said, smiling down
with that tender, soothing gesture. "I call Harry
that, sometimes — Harry Fortune. He's *un*fortunate enough in some things, poor fellow! But he
is handsome and good, and he has the loveliest light
hair, like yours. I haven't found any one before
that I wanted to speak to about *him* since I came
East — and I love him so! I hunger to see him so!
You make me think of him. He is so brave and
bright, and always running into some danger and
getting hurt, and then his eyes look as happy and
dreamy over it as though they'd never waked up.
He's poor, and he works in papa's mills; and he
hasn't any relatives; and he saved some people once,
when the dam broke down, and got awfully hurt,
and walks a little lame ever since ; and he made an
invention and somebody stole it ; and so on, and
so on ; but still his eyes keep dreaming and smiling on as though they'd never waked up.

"I'm engaged to him, and papa knows it. And
papa thinks everything of him in the mills ; but a
man is different, and I suppose when papa sent me
East to be cultured he thought I might forget
Harry Fortune. But not all the teachers and
schools between the two oceans could ever culture
my heart away from Harry Fortune."

Dick had been inclined to feel a little jealous when Harry Fortune's name was introduced, but as she looked up into Dakotah's brave, shining eyes, where the tears shone, too, at the same time, a generous sympathy glowed in her heart.

"I want you to make my room your home, little girl," said Dakotah, brightly, brushing away the tears. "I have a room quite to myself. I brought a note from a physician saying that I must have more air. But air and sunlight and breeze, you bring them all in with you, Dick. Come to me whenever you can."

As Dick stepped out into the hall, the vision of that plenteous grace and beauty and love still followed her. To be womanly! To know how to sew — how deftly the white fingers had mended her dress! To be so gracious! To sit so tranquil and still! To love unselfishly! A sudden, vague, half-frightened yearning that had never been there before, crept into my Dick's wild heart.

On her way down the stairs Dick met the laughing Hawaii. Hawaii's face was full of a bright mystery. She led the way to a room where there was a musty odor, and various strange physiological specimens lying about, and, in the centre, a mounted human skeleton.

Dick had always had an idea, in a general sort of way, that her own fair flesh covered bones, but she had never before gazed upon this unmitigated aspect of the human frame. A singular fascination drew her nearer to it; she touched it cautiously with the tip of her finger, and then withdrew a little.

"Who was it?" she whispered to Hawaii.

Hawaii enjoyed the situation. "She was a teacher," she answered, mysteriously; "and she all dried up."

"Oh!" said Dick.

"Do they keep it to try dresses on?" Dick asked, presently.

"No," said Hawaii; "she's a model."

"Oh!" said Dick, again.

Both of the young things now stood gazing at the skeleton, until, mingled with the awe on their faces, there came at last a strange hankering to possess.

"Do you suppose they want it for anything?" said Dick to Hawaii.

"No," said Hawaii; "it was just shut up in here all alone."

Dick thought another space. "I should like to

put it in the closet to take my 'half-hours,'" she said. "It's awfully cold and dark in there, but *she* wouldn't mind now, you know."

" No," said Hawaii ; "*she* wouldn't mind."

Silently Dick and Hawaii carried the skeleton through the now empty halls. F. Armenia Stetson and B. Arabella Bell were both absent at their recitations ; so the skeleton-bearers passed bravely on their unimpeded progress through the room, and deposited their precious burden in the closet. They then returned to their quest for entertainment in the halls, with the air of those whom one bright discovery has inspired with boundless hope. They did not know that the solemn bell for study-hours had pealed through Mount Grimrood Seminary ; that most of the pupils were in the various class-rooms at their recitations ; that the juniors (among whom they were properly classed) were undergoing their examinations in the seminary hall. But they were discovered at last, and led in to the ordeal, Dick stationed at one extreme of the hall and Hawaii at the other, and their examination papers given to them. The first was Arithmetic, the answers to be written. Dick gazed at the enigmatical sheet with much wonder and some curiosity. Hawaii, who had solved her problems in a trice, watched from afar. The guardian teachers on the throne did not notice, among the many bowed heads, the sudden, swift, silent, and entire disappearance of Hawaii's bright head. Down on the floor of the seminary hall, down under the feet of the wondering juniors, noiselessly, steadily, hand over hand, Hawaii crept with her copy of written answers to Dick's relief.

CHAPTER X.

DICK'S LAST HOPE—IN AFRICA.

DICK began to find life at Mount Grimrood Seminary not without its spice and entertainment. There was not, to be sure, the noble and healthful exhilaration about it that there had been in riding her horse and rowing her boat at Dymsbury Park, but it gave room for infinite speculation and a wide variety of tactics. There was the secret enticing consciousness that, at every step, she was overpassing the barrier of some mysterious rule. Then she discovered within herself a supernatural aptness for detecting the still approach of Miss Calvin, Miss Ratting, and Miss Bean, and secured an equal development in the faculty of flight. She met the laughing Hawaii at every turn, and boldly and without any soft affectation of regret, eluded the society of F. Armenia Stetson and B. Arabella Bell. When, at night, slumber held its brief sway over the senses of the studious B. Arabella, Dick stole softly from her couch, and fled to the reposeful arms of Dakotah West, in "forty-six."

All these things had given to my Dick, as she went in to devotions on her third morning at Mount Grimrood Seminary, an easy and conscious air of victory. The proceedings which followed fell on her like a thunderbolt. After the usual exercises there was a silence, and then an ominous clearing of Miss Milton's throat.

"Young ladies," the principal of Mount Grimrood began, with pall-like gravity ; "yesterday — during study hours — while we were all supposed — to be engaged — at our various quiet and appropriate tasks — our valuable skeleton — was wilfully and secretly abducted — from the physiological department — and carried, — young ladies, — for some time — we could discern not whither.

"This morning, — young ladies, — as our dear Miss Stetson approached her closet — for the purpose of taking her devotional half-hour — and abstractedly opened the door — she was shocked and appalled — on being encountered — by the unexpected apparition — of an unclothed — human skeleton. By an almost superhuman control of her nerves — she was prevented — from falling prostrate — on the floor. What might have been the effect — of this sudden shocking spectacle — upon the more delicate — organization — of our dear Miss Bell — we tremble, — young ladies, — to contemplate.

"But how shall we designate — this affair? And what term shall we properly — apply — to the miscreant? The wilful purloining of our skeleton, — what was it, — young ladies, — but abduction? And what a turbulent spirit — must dwell within that one — of our number — who could recklessly inflict — such a shock — upon the nerves — of a precious schoolmate!

"I must desire — that the perpetrator — or perpetrators — of this act — appear — at my private apartment — immediately — after this exercise."

Again Dick passed out of the Seminary Hall beneath the suspicious and condemnatory gaze of many eyes. "Abductor! Perpetrator!" the many eyes seemed to say, with dark and criminal significance. "Abductor! Perpetrator!"

Dakotah West was making desperate wafts of air with her fan, as she drew Dick into a little passageway in the outer hall. "It was *you*, of course — oh, my Towhead!" said she.

"Oh, Dakotah," said Dick, impulsively; "I didn't think of stealing their old skeleton—and I didn't do it to frighten that Bean girl or that Stetson girl, either."

"What *did* you do it for, oh, my Towhead?" said Dakotah.

"Because," said Dick; "I'd never seen one before, and I wanted to look at it some more; and besides—oh, Dakotah! it was so chilly and dark in that closet, and I put it in there to take my 'half-hours.'"

Dakotah dropped her fan, and sank breathless on the floor. "Go, immortal one!" she gasped; "go, and confess your crime! Oh, when will those unfathomable eyes of yours awaken to the ways of this little world? But come to my room afterwards, forgiven or unforgiven, for I had a beautiful box of goodies arrive this morning, and you shall find consolation."

Dick proceeded on her way to the tribunal, expecting every moment to overtake Hawaii; but, for once, the bright form of Hawaii was not visible, neither was she in Miss Milton's room when Dick arrived there. Dick was disappointed, not so much because she wanted a companion in disgrace, as that one whom she held so dear and brave as Hawaii should offend against the simple code of honor which had ever prevailed at Dymsbury Park.

"Did you carry — the skeleton — to your room — *alone?*" said Miss Milton, in the course of her earnest remonstrance with Dick.

Dick was true to the code. Under the circumstances she would have considered it more honorable to tell a hundred lies than to implicate the recreant Hawaii.

Miss Milton then proposed a day of solitary confinement for Dick. She was to be locked in her room and remain there, contemplative, fasting, until supper time. "And furthermore," said Miss Milton; "you must never — appear again among your schoolmates — with your hair — in that loose and wanton — condition. You must confine it — to your head — in some decorous — and appropriate — manner."

As Dick passed out of Miss Milton's room, she instantly encountered the merry eyes of Hawaii, peering out at her from behind a safe post of observation. "I thought I wouldn't go in," said Hawaii. "I knew you wouldn't tell. And I knew it wouldn't make so much difference with you. *You* ain't going to be a missionary, you know."

Dick's clear eyes met Hawaii's without reproach, as she passed on to her doom. A messenger was soon sent by Miss Milton, and Dick's door was locked on the outside. In vain Hawaii lingered about outside — but when Dick heard the retreat of the beloved Dakotah's footsteps, her heart sank. The dinner-hour approached. Hungry and sad, Dick was leaning out of the window, when she felt a touch on her shoulder. It was a basket let down by Dakotah from an empty recitation-room some stories above. Dick looked up. Dakotah was beaming down upon her, from that height, like an angel; but she put her fingers to her lips. If Dick had known, this sort of communication was a terrible infraction on the laws of Mount Grimrood; but in the happiness of the moment she never thought of referring to her long list of faithfully copied rules. The basket contained oranges, sweet crackers, sponge-cake, and a nearly upright pitcher of lemonade. Dick unloaded it with a grateful heart, and Dakotah drew it up empty, — save for a little inky message of love and thanksgiving, which she, however, put away, smiling, as though she considered it something quite precious. The basket descended again with words of consolation, and repeated its upward journey with buoyancy, containing large expressions of hope ; and in this sweet communication an hour passed quickly. Refreshed, Dick was enabled to deliberate cheerfully whether she should now compose herself to write a sermon, or a letter to Excelluna. She finally decided on the latter course, and indited such a long and picturesque account of the situation at Mount Grimrood Seminary as, on reperusal, made a really glowing appeal to her own sympathies. But when she considered how it would cause fond Excelluna to weep and wonder, and wrestle, all tearful and alone, with the powers of darkness, she tore it up and wrote a few short lines instead, telling her how she thought, all the time, of her and dear Dymsbury Park, and how she thought she was getting toned down very fast at Mount Grimrood. This done, she was surprised to find how near it was to the time of her release. She bethought her of what Miss Milton had said about her hair ; that she must never appear with it again in a wanton condition, but must confine it somehow to her head.

Dick wandered to the glass and ruminated vaguely. Then her eyes fell upon Miss Bell's curling-irons, and she remembered how a certain Miss Ratting, among the teachers at Mount Grimrood, whose hair also was light, wore a tight coil at the nape of the neck and three curls at each ear. Dick remembered how, as Miss Ratting walked, the wiry blonde curls bobbed methodically up and down ; and now, with a definite object and ideal in view, she set herself to work to imprison her own silken mane. So absorbed she grew in this novel and almost exciting pursuit she could hardly realize that another hour had passed when she heard the supper-bell peal through the hall, and, a moment afterwards, the withdrawing of the bolt in her door. Taking a last sidelong glance in the glass, as she passed out, Dick saw with satisfaction that the golden coil in her neck, though ragged and turbulent-looking, was firmly secured ; and that the six cruelly heated and unnatural curls stuck out stiffly from her head, and that, as she walked, — unconsciously assuming something of Miss Ratting's sedate and measured tread — they bobbed methodically up and down.

Dick had grown so used by this time to having

her advent, on any occasion, heralded by a mysterious silence, that the impressive stillness which instantly prevailed as she entered the dining-hall caused her little surprise. With an increased stateliness of tread, which caused a still loftier dance of the dreadful curls, she passed on to her seat; when suddenly, from the other end of the room, there arose, in a voice which she recognized as Hawaii's, an irrepressible shrill scream of glee, followed, from the quarter where Dakotah sat fanning herself, by ripple after ripple of perfectly spontaneous laughter. That wild scream of delight, those helpless ripples of laughter, spread like a contagion through the dining-hall of Mount Grimrood Seminary, and echoed from lip to lip. At this auspicious moment Dick's heart bounded with hope. She was about to propose an insurrection on the spot — when the mirth subsided, and she was led quietly away by Miss Milton herself. The effect of the day's solitary confinement upon Dick had not been such as Miss Milton had hoped for.

After a certain number of infringements on the rules of Mount Grimrood, it was written, the pupil's relation with that institution must cease. It appeared that Dick had already far passed the goal, but she bore the news that her probation was virtually at an end with such unaffected, even cheerful resignation, that Miss Milton concluded, in view of so peculiar and urgent a case, and the unfortunate circumstances attending Dick's early training, to give her one more trial.

There came at about this time, as Dick remembers, to Mount Grimrood Seminary a week in which the lessons, all secular duties, were given up, and the long hours devoted to exclusively religious meetings in the large hall and in the parlors. Under the protracted solemnity of the time, Dick's unawakened soul was filled with a horrible wonder. But the laughing Hawaii, of a different nature, succumbed at last to the strange influence.

That Hawaii was *going to be good* struck Dick as a mournful, even a tragic circumstance. Her friend's blue eyes, when she met her now, though smiling, were strange and subdued, often suffused with tears. She waited for Dick no more in all forbidden places between the cupola and the basement, nor ever called to her gayly again from her perch on the banisters ; and at last Dick missed her face in the public places of the school, at devotions, and at the table. Then she heard that Hawaii had been taken ill and had been removed to the " sick ward." Poor Dick honestly believed that it was all in consequence of her friend's conversion, and a nameless dread and bitterness crept into her heart. She thought, too, that Hawaii would die; and that had meant something beautiful at Dymsbury Park, Excelluna had discovered, through her far-offs, — but to die, at Mount Grimrood! Dick shuddered. She wandered much up and down the halls, disappearing deftly at the approach of the teachers, a pitifully desolate and hunted look on her face, nor in her despair would even go to the loving Dakotah for comfort.

A missionary from Africa came to preach at Mount Grimrood Seminary. He preached two long sermons with weary statistics, which the pupils were requested to copy. In the evening he preached again, but this time it was a personal appeal to the young women of Mount Grimrood to leave their native land, homes, friends, expecta· tions, to carry the torch of salvation into benighted Africa. A box was to be left on a window-shelf in the Seminary Hall, and, ere the retiring bell rang that night, those who would leave all to go on the mission were to drop their names on a slip of paper in the box.

Dick had listened intently. The description of the unfettering costumes, the free and easy manners, the wild, out-of-door life of the original heathen caused, Dick confessed to herself, with a guilty sort of ecstasy, a kindred chord to vibrate in her own bosom. It appeared to her that by joining herself ostensibly to the missionaries she might, on her arrival at the shores of Africa, escape into the happy and enticing borders of the heathen. At all events it seemed to be preferable to remaining at Mount Grimrood Seminary. She wrote her name on a slip of paper, and, as the poor moth hovers, fascinated though half unwilling, about the destroying flame, so Dick drew ever nearer and nearer to that mysterious box. Then, through the little chink at the top, she dropped in her name. There was no withdrawing it. Miss Milton alone held the key that unlocked that dark treasury. Dick dropped in her name, turned, stood one moment with wild eyes, then put her hands to her ears and fled from the room.

As the retiring bell rang, the missionary box was brought to Miss Milton. She opened it and read the names.　At one name she gave a quick start of surprise.　Then a flush as of some good triumph or delight overspread her features.　"Poor child!" she murmured; "she has been touched at last, and in her blind, childlike, impetuous way, she, too, longs to devote herself to the great work."　With that one little slip of paper in her hand, the principal of Mount Grimrood rose to find Dick.　Passing through the dim Seminary Hall, she paused suddenly before a shock of light hair and a prostrate form stretched on one of the wooden benches.　It was even the object of her search, desolate, wandering Dick herself.　But Miss Milton did not stop then to remonstrate.

"I was on my way—to your room—my child," she said, sitting down at Dick's head

Dick raised herself, looking like an animal at bay.

"I wanted to tell you," Miss Milton went on, "what a happy surprise—it gave me—to find your name—in the box.　You are so young—we cannot yet—accept the sacrifice.　But did it really seem to you—that you would like to join us—in our missionary work?"

Dick laughed.　It was half a laugh and half a

dry, defiant sob. Dick, though she had sometimes suffered, had not yet learned how to cry.

"Let the tears come — poor child. It is good for us — sometimes. It is a relief," said Miss Milton's weary voice.

"I never cry!" retorted Dick, quite savagely.

"And did it really — seem to you — that you would like — to join us — in our missionary work?" Miss Milton patiently repeated.

"No!" said Dick, with perfect recklessness; "it was because I thought, if I went out there, I might get a chance to join the heathen!"

"Is it so!" Miss Milton answered gently, without a shadow of rebuke in her tone. "Is it so — is it so;" she slowly repeated to herself. The strange quietness of her tone touched Dick. "I have been thinking," Miss Milton continued; "I may not always — have understood — my dear. You were left motherless — I have been a homeless, childless woman — I have dealt generally — with trained minds. My heart yearns over you — but my position was one — of care and responsibility for so many. You will forgive me — I am so tired — it is hard for me to speak. It will all be well — in the end."

As Miss Milton uttered these disconnected sentences in her broken, impressive tone of voice, Dick crept nearer to her and even put out a hand to touch her dress.

"I could not bear the excitement — it would have caused — had I announced my intention — to the school," Miss Milton went on. "I am going away — to-morrow. I am going — with the expedition — to help in the founding — of a school in Africa. Miss Calvin — will take my place — here. It will all — be well."

Miss Milton's broken voice again failed her, and Dick's hand crept up softly to the principal of Mount Grimrood's knees. "If I ever return," said Miss Milton; "it will not be — for long years to come. I am tired — but I am calm — to-night. I believe it will all — be well. Promise me that you will go to your room now. I shall not see you again — dear child. Good night — good-bye."

But Dick had drawn very close to Miss Milton. With wondering pity she lifted up both cool hands and stroked the hollow, feverish cheeks. Then, because it seemed to her that it would comfort the principal of Mount Grimrood, she put her lips to them with kisses.

Amazed at this final, strange capture of the prodigal, the principal of Mount Grimrood, with an almost passionate yearning and regret strained Dick to her heart.

CHAPTER XI.

EXPELLED.

A S the inflexible Miss Calvin ascended the throne vacated by Miss Milton, Dick had a quiet and perfectly secure consciousness that her days at Mount Grimrood were numbered.

Every morning, with her fan in one hand and her botanical box in the other, Dakotah West swept splendidly out of the halls of Mount Grimrood. Something in Dakotah's presence impressed the teacher who granted her this unusual permission with the feasibility of the plan, implying, as it seemed to, large researches and possible new discoveries in the botanical realm. Dick, professing a similar *penchant*, had frequently obtained, under Miss Milton's rule, a similar permission; but her saunterings were now legally restricted to a walk to the "Half-mile post," a simple slab which marked the ordinary close of the digressions of the pupils of Mount Grimrood. Dick's egress, therefore, was made through a narrow window in the basement, where she crept out unobserved and sped like a deer across the fields.

Dick and Dakotah met at a clump of pine-trees just out of sight of the seminary walls. There, in waiting, with his quaint country horse and wagon, stood a simple, good-natured lad of the village, by name Neddie Farmer. Him had my Dick and Dakotah approached one day in the fields as a rare and deserving specimen, and had invited him to employ his fascinating equipage in carrying them about country at a commission far greater than he was accustomed to earn at the plough. Neddie Farmer at last consented. Though himself of a highly mirthful temperament, he seemed to regard the conduct of these two young ladies as mysteriously wild and doubtful, and deemed it necessary to assume in their presence some shining intention of being sedate. But neither the tall hat of antique shape nor the lugubrious black coat which he wore while driving them could put an entire check on his native propensities. He replied to any remark of theirs with the utmost reserve and circumspection, but could not help exclaiming delightedly, on occasion, "There's a chip-munk!" After which they saw his ears beneath his tall hat pitifully suffused with blushes.

But it was in view of a wayside-well that all righteousness forsook Neddie Farmer. He was accustomed to leap from the wagon, unloose the bucket, and, as it went madly clattering on its way down the well, spring back to his seat and apply the lash to his horse. Nor could the sombre aspect of his hugely enveloping hat conceal the deep smile which played on his features as he looked back to see the startled housewives shaking their brooms and mops at him in the distance. It was partly, no doubt, on account of this playful habit of Neddie Farmer's that the party found it more agreeable to drive in a new direction each day. Among the fresh breezes on the hills, Dakotah temporarily laid aside her fan and expanded to the full her starving chest, and Dick was supremely happy.

One evening, alighting, as was their wont, at the clump of pine-trees, they started suddenly to see an irate and fantastic figure rising out of the brush. It was the ringleted Miss Bean, who had been lying in wait for them, and whose worst suspicions were now verified.

That he considered it, in somebody's case at

least, as a remarkable instance of letting the bucket down the well, was evident by the speed with which Neddie Farmer turned his horse about and put out for the main road.

"I suppose you know the result of this conduct, young ladies," said Miss Bean, in tones as clear and cold as fate. "It is, I can confidently assure you, nothing less than *expulsion.* You have been discovered driving outside the seminary grounds. You have been discovered, young ladies, driving *with a man !*"

Having thus pronounced the crack of doom over those two young heads, Miss Bean turned and walked rapidly towards the house.

Dick and Dakotah followed thoughtfully.

"So Neddie Farmer's hat and coat have produced an effect at last," murmured Dakotah. "With a *man !* Truly these cloistered souls are indiscriminate ! But you see, there's the rub. *With a man !* Expelled we shall be, sure enough. And I should hate to decline the honor. Already, my sweetest Towhead, I begin to breathe. But first the teachers will have to spend a day in solemn conclave, and then there will be a series of meetings appointed, in a last effort for our misguided souls, and meantime, oh my Dick——"

"I know," said Dick, with sudden eager animation. "It isn't for nothing I used to play I was a boy sometimes at Dymsbury Park. And I've got my regimentals with me."

Dick whispered in Dakotah's ear. Dakotah sank weakly a moment by the wayside; then rose with tears in her eyes.

"You're so tall, and your nose is such a perfectly elegant shape, you might do it!" she said. "Which are you going to take? Which are you going to make love to?"

"I shall take Miss Bean," answered Dick.

Later in the evening, the door-bell of Mount Grimrood Seminary rang with a sharp, elastic peal. The door-girl, with mingled wonder and admiration, ushered into the solitary reception-room a slight but distinguished-looking and strangely fascinating youth. The loose locks from his brown wig fell over a clear, white forehead. His large, golden-brown eyes gazed with singular directness through a pair of eye-glasses, which bestrode with charming effect his spirited and purely aristocratic nose, while a mustache, also of a golden hue, dropped over his exquisitely moulded lips. But when he opened those sweet lips and showed his white teeth and sighed; "Will you present this to Miss Bean?" the door-girl took his card, upon which was inscribed the name of Reginald De Monterey, and courtesied with an involuntary accent of approval.

Miss Bean entered the room with an agitated air and a smile of coy and unnatural sweetness: "Mr. De Monterey," she began, as the exquisite youth arose and cordially grasped her hand; " I do not exactly recall — I am happy, I'm sure — I do not remember —— "

"What!" impetuously exclaimed Reginald De Monterey. "Do not remember the friend of your childish school-days! The little Reggie who drew you on his sled, who helped you over the stile, who —— "

"Oh, indeed!" simpered Miss Bean, "the name — yes, certainly — the name, yes, I think it begins to grow familiar. But how — how you have changed, Mr. — a — Mr. De Monterey!"

"*You* have not changed," sighed Reginald De Monterey, putting his hand to his chin with an air of dejected, almost desperate musing.

"Pray be seated,.Mr. De Monterey," said Miss Bean.

"Ah, it was natural that you should forget!" said De Montercy, recklessly throwing himself into a chair. "How could I suppose, having carried your sweet image with me from childhood, that a similar regard had been awakened and cherished in your own bosom! It was madness. I have sought you out and found you at last in vain. Wealth, fame, the cold approval of the world — I have gained them all, and they are all as nothing to me, for it seems M. Edna Bean has forgotten me!" De Monterey again rose and rapidly paced the floor.

Miss Bean's numerous ringlets seemed fairly to quiver with excitement. "But certainly I begin to remember," said she — "and the eyes — I begin — certainly, I begin to recall them ——"

"Has forgotten me!" repeated De Monterey, as though he had not heard, still pacing the floor. "I confess, Miss Bean — since I may not call you by the old fond name — that I came to this quiet village purposely to find you out. I have observed you here at church; yes, and in your solitary walks among the pines, — nay, do not start, angelic creature! you could not deny me that brief privilege. And I have seen the beauty and purity which I adored in the child only blooming into a richer and more perfectly bewildering development in the maiden. The fond hope crept into my heart, seeing so much beauty ungathered, that you too cherished an image! Otherwise it seemed to me it could not be."

Miss Bean put her hand to her mouth and coughed, for some moments, with extreme nervousness.

"It cannot be," plaintively cried De Monterey, "that the fell destroyer of our northern clime has found you! that Death has chosen you for his bride! You are not consumptive!"

"Oh, no! no! no, indeed, Mr. De Monterey," gasped Miss Bean.

"It is well," said De Monterey; "may the life that is not to bless mine long shed its fragrance for others. Better had it been for *me* had I stayed away. Has forgotten me! Farewell, M. Edna Bean; but, remember, there is one who will never forget *you.* Farewell."

"Pray, pray do not be so disconsolate, Mr. De Monterey," cried Miss Bean, rising. "Do not, do not despair."

"What!" exclaimed De Monterey, turning with

passionate abruptness; "you bid me not **to** despair. You, M. Edna Bean — do you, do you bid me hope?"

"Oh, no, no, indeed! That is, yes, yes, Mr. De Monterey. Hush! the retiring bell! I must go! I must, indeed!"

"But say that you will meet me to-morrow — at the pines."

"I — oh — that is — yes — *I*, I will," whispered Miss Bean, and vanished like an uneasy ghost.

Reginald De Monterey passed out of the door and then crept along under the shadow of the house to the basement window, through which Dakotah West received him to her arms. "You are a perfect little Adonis!" said she. "But, oh, what would Harry Fortune think to see me taking you in through this window? And did the Bean prove impressionable?"

"She will meet me clandestinely at the pines to-morrow," flashed Dick through her white teeth, her eyes gleaming dark with merriment at Dakotah.

Dakotah struggled desperately with her emotions as she put the brown wig and moustache in her pocket, and assisted Dick in putting on her gown. "*Are* we sinful, my darling?" said she. "But she was *so* sly and cruel."

"I love it!" cried Dick, absently, in her enthusiasm; "I love to act anything! It comes to me just what to say, and it comes to me just what to do, but I wish, oh, Dakotah, I wish——"

"Wish what, dearest Towhead?"

"I just wish I'd gone for Miss Calvin, instead."

"Hush!" screamed Dakotah West.

Dakotah West watched from a nook among the shadowy pines the meeting of Miss Bean with Reginald De Monterey on the morrow. Dakotah marvelled solemnly at the strange self-abandonment of Dick's manner, at the inspired harmony of all her actions, the fire and freedom and grace. "She is a natural-born artist," whispered Dakotah to herself, and dropped her fan, wondering more and more, and drank in the proceedings, open-mouthed.

But when, invited by him to a sylvan seat, Miss Bean's head at last fell gently over and rested against Reginald De Monterey's bosom, the situation was too much for Dakotah West. Her inward appreciation of the scene escaped her in a confused but rapturous giggle, which crept through the gloomy solitude of the pines and smote upon the ears of the amorous couple.

"We are discovered!" cried Miss Bean, as she sprang to her feet; and, casting one wild, apprehensive glance about her, she fled from the place like a frightened doe.

"It was *I* who discovered you in the woods," said Dakotah West, overtaking the agonized Miss Bean in the halls of Mt. Grimrood. "Do not be frightened; your secret is known only to me and my friend Dick Bodurtha, and is perfectly safe."

A wretched compunction filled Miss Bean's breast. "There might have been," she said, "in your own case, when I discovered you, the other day, palliating circumstances which, —— "

"You gave us up to headquarters immediately, of course?" said Dakotah.

"I considered it my duty at the time. Possibly not understanding, I —— "

"It is all right," said Dakotah West. "We've got the screw on you, you little fool, but we don't care to use it. Your secret is perfectly safe."

Miss Bean winced. Whether from that miserable compunction or because she doubted so much magnanimity on the part of the two girls, she took pains to give out, that possibly — nay, that she was convinced that she had made a mistake in supposing the two young ladies whom she had recently discovered driving with a man, to be pupils of Mt. Grimrood Seminary. It could not be, however, but that Dick and Dakotah's fate was sealed. It was written on the face of the inexorable Miss Calvin; and Miss Bean was secretly glad.

It was the last time that Dick and Dakotah were ever to sit at devotions in the seminary hall, though the grand *dénouement* came, indeed, from an unexpected source. Dick gazed up dreamily at Miss Calvin, as she sat reading the chapter, on the throne; and, to her young imagination, that lifted face was as the stone upon which Moses had written the commandments long ago; the great black eyes seemed pitiless. Suddenly, Dick became aware that this solemn exercise was closed, and she waited indifferently through the long moment of breathless suspense which she had learned to know so well.

"Young ladies," then said the grave and awful voice of Miss Calvin, on the throne. "Young ladies; that we may with the greater ease and quietness walk about these halls, in mutual consideration for you and for each other, the teachers of

Mount Grimrood Seminary are accustomed to wear soft and unsqueaking shoes.

"But it appears, young ladies, that there are some of your number whose deeds are such that they wish to be informed of our approach ! They take no pleasure in being surprised by a visit from their faithful teachers, but would even wish to reinforce themselves against the possibility of such an accident !

"This morning, young ladies, there were found, forcibly implanted in the soles of our dear Miss Ratting's shoes, a quantity of *nails*, —young ladies, — of heavy and resounding *nails !*

"I will not stop, young ladies, to remark upon the character of this deed or its inevitable consequences. It is sufficient to ask the perpetrators, here in the presence of their school-mates and teachers, to rise."

Dick alone knew the secret of the nails. Twice had she discovered Miss Ratting, after a noiseless approach, listening surreptitiously at her door, and, in putting the nails in the soles of her shoes, she had taken such precautions as would have been deemed only just and expedient by all the spirits of Dymsbury Park. And now, for the last time, in the midst of the three hundred and sixty pupils, and before the forty teachers on the throne, Dick arose. But as she did so, another form was seen stately to rise in a distant part of the hall — a presence that stood sweetly, though arduously fanning itself — the magnificent Dakotah West. Across the three hundred and sixty heads Dick shot a glance of glowing love and admiration and rebuke, and opened her lips to speak, but Dakotah made an unmistakable, earnest sign of entreaty.

"Young ladies," said Miss Calvin to those two marked figures; "your relations as pupils of Mount Grimrood Seminary are *at an end*. Your friends have been written to, and will duly inform us whither to send you next. Meantime, you may remain with us as our dishonored, though com-passionated guests."

But Dick and Dakotah availed themselves of this last privilege for a period of time singularly brief. Through Neddie Farmer, procured to their assistance with wagon and ropes, the night wit-nessed the descent of their baggage and their own safe escape, and morning saw Dakotah West jour-neying happily westward, through freer currents of air, and my Dick, all daring and alone, *en route* for Dymsbury Park.

Excelluna sat in the porch of the old house at Dymsbury Park; the sun and wind were playing freely with her grizzled locks, but Excelluna's face was placid, — she was making flowers. At one hand she had a box of tinted paper, some shears and glue. Through her "fur-offs" she caught the inspiration, and through her "nigh-tos" she constructed the flowers. "Some have said to me," Excelluna murmured pensively to herself, "that there *be not* no sech flowers as these that I am makin'. 'Where be they?' says they; and they have sometimes laughed" — Excelluna's tone was even compassionate — "'where be they?' says they. 'We have never seen no sech flowers!' But" — and here Excelluna adjusted her fur-offs and took a long, rapturous gaze into the Elysian fields — "there air, maybe, more flowers than is ginerally thought on. *I*," said Excelluna "*have seen sech flowers,*" and she replaced her nigh-tos, and worked studiously on a crimson-lined lily with a golden-green chalice.

But a dear, familiar step came down the walk. Quickly Excelluna put on her spectacles of spiritual vision, and gazed, and gazed, while no surprise came to her face; only the same quiet, beatified expression. "It is ever and a darlin' one," said Excelluna ; but so had she seen her many times every day since that morning she had gone away. When Dick threw her arms emphatically about the old woman's neck, and called her "Luny! Dear old Luny!"—"It is, it is, indeed! Heving be praised!" said Excelluna ; but soon she touched the darling of her heart softly and curiously again as though it had been a blessed ghost.

Dick ran wildly about the house and farm. Her horse, her boat, the young Pinchons, all belonging to Dymsbury Park, she embraced with an indiscriminate gladness. But there was just the slightest change in her darling's manner which set the old serving-woman at last to a weary, earthly speculation. Dick told the story of her career at Mount Grimrood with thrilling dash and effect, and an indescribable arch mimicry. There was a little inclination to jeer, an occasional flavor of bitterness now in the sweet laugh ; and when she went to bed that night she did not kneel down to say the prayer Excelluna had taught her. Excelluna recounted the lively narrative. Very tranquil and beautiful Dick looked as she lay asleep ; but . Excelluna stood in the shadows, a deeper care shadowed on her brow, her finger pressed in a sad thoughtfulness against her lips: "*The toning down,*" slowly said Excelluna, "*do not appear to be sech as was thought on.*"

Excelluna retired to her bedroom, and by the faint light of a candle endeavored to peruse her Fox's Book of Martyrs; but for once that dear chronicle yielded her no comfort. After another hour of distracting restlessness she sought her bottle of paregoric, and applied the extreme tip of her finger to that guileless mixture. "I know it ain't a cure," said Excelluna; "I have sometimes thought it was a help." It was hardly a help that night.

But sleep came at last to that poor troubled heart; and then indeed Excelluna saw a garden to which all the visions of her day-dreams were but as a hint and a beginning. And as she looked, through blooms purple and red, into a white, white field, smiling walked the darling of her heart.

A childlike peace had smoothed all the wrinkles from Excelluna's brow. She smiled; a happy tear stole down her check. "*I,*" she murmured softly in her sleep, "*have seen sech flowers.*"

CHAPTER XII.

PERSONAL SUPERVISION.

ON receiving the news from Mount Grimrood Seminary Mrs. Bodurtha showed a face almost pathetic in its cold dismay. But when she spoke at last there was a keen determination in her utterance. "I shall now," she said, "take my niece, for a time at least, under my personal care and supervision. I am sure, even with my shrinking from, and incapacity for the task, nothing worse can happen than has happened. Instead of coming to me my sister's child fled immediately to Dymsbury Park. There is a horrible fatality about that place. Oh, why did I ever send her there!"

Mrs. Bodurtha submitted herself gloriously to the wave of determination and self-sacrifice which swept over her. She returned from her summer saunterings a week earlier than was her wont — though the weather had grown prematurely chill —

and established herself in the house in town ready for her niece's reception.

Mr. Higgins, Dick's guardian, the venerable Crœsus, who, though always affable and indulgent, Dick with a constant instinct defied, came to lure my young lady from her wild retreat to her aunt's polished abode. Dick at first flatly refused to go, and her guardian laughingly encouraged her in this fine audacity, just as he had been used to play with the temper of the wilful and engaging child. He smilingly suggested that, though she might prefer to take up her permanent abode at Dymsbury Park, she would find it vastly entertaining to spend a week or two in the city. In the same smooth, caressing tone, he further suggested that she should take her favorite horse with her, as she "would find it delightful riding in the park, attended, of course, by a groom." This found at once the mysterious key of Dick's affections and pleased her imagination. She consented to try the adventure.

But very soon after her arrival at New York the girl was stricken down with a long and feverish illness. Often then she moaned for Excelluna; but Mrs. Bodurtha shuddered at the name, and the ancient serving-woman never knew how near her darling came at that time to death's door.

In the real danger and suffering of her illness, Dick was so brave, so sweet, that Mrs. Bodurtha, to whom this was a strange revelation of the girl's character, was genuinely alarmed. She had always had hitherto a certain unexpressed security in the feeling that Dick was too sinful to die. She suddenly realized how precious was the life of this last branch of a worthy family, the young life hanging now by so slender a thread. She waited, pale, faithful, anxious in and about the sick-room, and when Dick began to mend, the little world about her, Mrs. Bodurtha included, was at her feet.

The days of my young lady's recovery were filled with every conceivable attention and indulgence. The sharp-eyed female who had been employed to correct her manners and education, was not re-called, even when all the former elasticity had come back to Dick's tread, and the healthiest color to her cheeks. As for her manners, Dick could not help seeing that they were now generally conceded to be, though sometimes erratic, of the most charming and interesting character; and as for her education, "The child shall not be confined to her books again," said Mrs. Bodurtha, gravely, "for a long time to come."

Dick sojourned alternately with her aunt, and at the still more sumptuous residence of her guardian, on the avenue. The latter resort was often filled with fashionable guests, who also made a pet of Dick, especially certain women of *le beau monde*, who spared no pains to instruct her as to the full worth of charms hitherto but half known or appreciated, as well as how to apply them in the most striking and fascinating manner.

The servants, the equipages, the grand dinners, the private box at the theatre, the novelty and splendor of · this life appealed to Dick's young senses and rich imagination. She threw herself into it with head and heart as into a bewitching play. Her eyes shone and her cheeks flushed with pleasure as she watched the effect of new and exquisite toilets in the glass. The little brown hands that had found such simple delight in the pleasures of Dymsbury Park grew white and fastidious enough. The shock of "wanton" hair was dressed with charming effect.

And at the play, amid fair scenery and brilliant lights and strains of enchanting music, there was the panorama of passion and romance, often the laughing triumph of the worldly sentiment, the covert sneer, the insidious word. The fire of the gay scene crept into Dick's brain. She carried it into the restless round of her pleasure-seeking life. Very far off now grew all the voices of Dymsbury Park. Very far away indeed, was Excelluna, making her celestial flowers in the sunlight.

In a vain and unscrupulous treatment of the youth who paid homage to her charms, in a sweet-tempered indocility, a perfectly self-possessed reck-lessness and hauteur, the unconscious girl, as nat-urally as though it had been a part of some former life to which she had come back for a season, transcended the teachings of her gay and worldly companions.

Mrs. Bodurtha realized a new danger. She spoke anxiously to Mr. Higgins: "It is unwise," said she, "it is even scandalous, the license we have allowed this child of seventeen. Of course her dangerous illness incapacitated her for immediate severe application to her studies, and we wished to have her amused; but she has taken her own head, until, though very sweet-tempered, she seems really to be amenable neither to God, nor reason, nor humanity! Physically, she is splendidly developed; but oh, Mr. Higgins,"—the lady gasped—"she is growing very headstrong, and I fear, I fear that she may still be *profoundly* ignorant!"

Mr. Higgins, too, was of the opinion that a quiet change was necessary for Dick. "Her love for the theatre and her young flirtations are amusing, but we must prevent her from taking any impetuous step," he said, blandly; "and especially in that matter of the theatre,—the—the mother's predilections, you know, my dear Mrs. Bodurtha, might, in time——"

Mr. Higgins tried to intimate a danger and to speak soothingly at the same time. Mrs. Bodurtha lifted her hand entreatingly; "I know, I know," she sighed.

"She is still too young, as you say," continued Mr. Higgins, "to be devoted wholly to society; still too young to consider seriously a question which I shall some time propose to her."

Mrs. Bodurtha started, but recovered herself immediately.

"It is my intention, my desire, my dear Mrs. Bodurtha," the guardian went on with unbroken smoothness and composure of tone; "to assume towards your niece the duties not only of the guardian and *quasi* father, but the authority and privileges of the *husband* as well. What say you?" he added, laughing softly. "My house is not an humble one, but I have a fancy that our spirited young lady will become it immensely."

And could it be, could it be — Mrs. Bodurtha could not help musing with triumph — that such a prospect as this was already opening before her niece! that, at seventeen, her hand should be desired by this polished possessor of millions, the long-coveted prize of a thousand drawing-rooms!

"While I have no doubt, dear Mr. Higgins," she answered gravely, "that your kind proposal would indeed insure the safest and happiest future that could be for my niece, still, we are both aware of the fact that that young lady sometimes exhibits, on the most inopportune occasions, an exceedingly perverse and determined will of her own."

"Fortunately, fortunately," responded Mr. Higgins, in a smiling manner, quite undismayed; "otherwise she would be extremely uninteresting. I think I shall succeed. And meantime, my dear

Mrs. Bodurtha, there certainly must be in her case an entire change of scene and companions. There must, indeed, be imposed a few months of devotion to quiet and studious pursuits. In our desire to advance her physical recovery we wholly let go the reins of government, and under present circumstances it is not easy to resume them. We could hardly establish now, under our personal direction, an entire change of life and conduct, or a system of studious application for your niece, without producing a misunderstanding and — a — a possible dislike and rebellion on her part, which would be — a — a — particularly undesirable. The good of our precious charge seems to make it imperative that we should again be separated from her for a season, and give her entirely to the care of other hands."

Mrs. Bodurtha lifted her eyes with veneration to the Crœsus. "It is the very thing," said she, "which I have been so anxiously contemplating."

"My next proposal," continued the suave voice, "will surprise you. I propose that we send our charge now, not to any of our fashionable boarding-schools, where she will be subjected to a false system of espionage, but to put her, just for a trial, mainly on her own conscience and mettle; to give her, in short, my dear Mrs. Bodurtha, a term amidst the struggle and ambition of a Western university!"

"A Western university?" palely echoed Mrs. Bodurtha.

"A Western university!" firmly but encouragingly reiterated Mr. Higgins. "In the university of 'The Three Lakes,' which I have largely endowed, in a lovely and healthful Western village our Miss Bodurtha will be far, far separated from the exciting scenes of the past few months; positively, my dear Mrs. Bodurtha," exulted the wise guardian, "positively out of dreaming distance of the theatre. Amongst a struggling and ambitious body of young people she will recognize her own deficiencies and do her utmost to remedy the mistake. I would propose a few months of it, only enough to set the mind quietly in a new direction, and to — a — a — apply a few fundamental facts in — a — a — various branches. And *then*, when she comes back, she shall renew her life here under the safe guardianship and protecting care of a mature, but, I trust, devoted husband."

The soft laugh which followed this remark awoke

Mrs. Bodurtha from a profound reverie. She lifted her head, speaking in a tone of solemn conviction. "I am perfectly assured," said she, "that this is, indeed, the best thing that can now be done."

Mrs. Bodurtha was taken aback by the calm, even hopeful manner in which Dick received the news of this new plan for her education. Mrs. Bodurtha did not know that just as Dick now sometimes found the play dull and lifeless, and looked through it to the stale end and wearied of it, so this new life was in truth seeming naught but a play also ; a brief fever and insanity, through which the clear eyes were already beginning to gaze, wearied, restless for something, they knew not what, — something deeper and beyond.

The Western land was golden and fair to Dick's imagination. Mrs. Bodurtha was chagrined by the cheerful and uncomplaining way in which her niece bade her good-bye. "The child is heartless !" she said, bitterly, as she turned away. "She has nothing but a beautiful body and a restless, untamable spirit. Her guardian thinks she may be subdued ; I hope to heaven she may be subdued ! "

The guardian accompanied Dick to her destination, saw her safely established in a commodious room in the "ladies' hall" at the University of the Three Lakes, and committed to the care of the excellent matron, and then, with some flowery words of parting advice and a generous bestowal in the way of pocket-money, he went away. Dick, it is true, felt no pangs at his departure either. This very unfortunate fortunate girl had never known the real sorrow of parting, the true, beautiful, childish anguish of homesickness. But when the tea-bell rang, and the merry girls poured out into the halls, laughing, shouting, and twining their arms about each other in strange contrast to the customs of Mt. Grimrood Seminary, as Dick followed alone in this strange land, a sudden, undefined sense of want, of possible injustice, filled her heart and eyes. Almost at the same instant there fell on her ears, in a fond, familiar voice, a scream of perfect delight, and she was caught up in a rapturous embrace. "Oh, my dearest, sweetest Towhead," rippled the sweet voice of Dakotah West in her ear, "*can* it be you?"

CHAPTER XIII.

WESTWARD, HO!

FROM an eminence the university buildings looked south, east, and west upon three lovely lakes.

On this broad and commanding height Dakotah West found the air sufficient to her needs. From the list of her various splendid appointments her fan had now entirely disappeared, while she drank in the divine nectar with such deep and joyous inspirations as only those who have suffered from aerial privation can truly know and appreciate.

"When papa heard about the air East, — that there wasn't any, you know—" she cheerfully explained to Dick; "he gave up the *culturing* business and said he would send me *now* where I would *learn* something. All the same, I know papa's design is to have me forget Harry Fortune; but I told him it wouldn't be of any use. Even if I should try," said Dakotah West, lifting her brave and tender eyes to Dick; "how could I ever forget my poor, dear, struggling boy?"

Dick still admired Dakotah, and was fond of her, and had the fullest faith in her sincerity, but she was not affected as she had once been by this simple exhibition of sentiment. The young girl gave a very breezy, incredulous laugh. "I think it is easier to forget people than to love them," she said.

"You have got some very vile ideas from somewhere, then," exclaimed Dakotah West, sadly, though with considerable warmth.

"I'd rather have those than silly ones," answered Dick.

Dakotah, thoroughly hurt, rose and went out. In less than an hour she returned, and, with tears in her handsome eyes, begged Dick's pardon. Dick was used to such a result in the various unimportant controversies in which she indulged, and readily pardoned Dakotah.

"Only I *don't* like silly talk," said she, with a slight shrug of the shoulders.

Dakotah quietly bit her lips. The honest girl's thoughts turned to something else. She sighed. "How about your lessons, Dick?" said she. "*I'm* taking an elective course, only just such branches as you please, you know."

"I will do that way, too," said Dick, with pleasing animation.

"*I* like it," said Dakotah West, with whom the easy application of written lore had never been, indeed, a conspicuous trait.

It seemed to be an occasion of unusual seriousness to the mind of the good-natured Dakotah. She spoke with a grave, engaging frankness. "I *can't* learn, Dick," she said. "It has been a source of great mortification to me, and I've tried again and again. I love to read. I love to observe. Thousands of things that I don't try to remember will stay by me constantly and forever. But the moment I sit down for the ostensible purpose of committing anything to my memory, my mind becomes a perfect blank, a perfect dim, boundless, soundless blank. Can you learn easily, Dick?"

"I don't know," said Dick, vaguely.

"You might try it, some time," gravely suggested Dakotah, "and see."

Dick's expression still continuing vague, Dakotah resumed:—

"I've taken up Botany this term, because — because I'm so used to it, for one thing, though there isn't really any need of it here. But it's in a beautiful recitation-room up on the fourth floor of the college building, where the view of the lakes is perfectly sublime. The class is a perfect hubbub of fun. I can't describe it to you ; but the teacher is a boyish-looking, conceited little sprig, and the fellows cut up awfully. There are about seventy girls and boys in the class. I sit in the back row, and the teacher doesn't often have time in the recitation-hour to get so far with a question. I don't think I've been asked a question in the Botany class for two weeks," said Dakotah, with calm and serious satisfaction.

"I shall take up Botany again," said Dick, emphatically.

"And then," continued Dakotah West, "I've taken up Anglo-Saxon besides," — Dakotah waited a moment, blushingly to observe what effect this pretentious and pedantic-sounding statement had upon Dick. She was encouraged by Dick's manner to proceed, — "It's the language, you know, dearest Towhead, that the old Anglo-Saxons used to converse to each other in — and it's simply horrible ; but the text-book is small, and easy to carry about ; and the recitation comes right after Botany, at the second hour in the morning, which gives you all the rest of the day for recreation unbroken ; and there are some of the nicest fellows in the university in the class ; though I don't accept serious attentions from any one but Harry,"—Dakotah paused again, with bright cheeks, gazing very directly and bravely at Dick,—"but I have some good friends among the boys."

"But what do you do about learning that horrid lesson, you know?" inquired Dick.

"Oh," said Dakotah, "Professor Dane is perfectly splendid. He's indifferent to everything but his work. He has worked his way up from poverty, they say, and some terrible family misfortune, I don't know what, and he's only thirty, and he's very distinguished already, and he's tall and stoops a little, and his hair is black and beginning to turn, and his eyes are perfectly killing."

"But how do you manage about the lesson, Dakotah?"

"Certainly, dear. Professor Dane is so high-minded and dignified, you know, he isn't forever on the lookout to catch somebody in a foolish little trick," said Dakotah, with singularly honest enthu-

siasm. • " In class, he invariably begins with Dan
Gaylord, and takes us right up, in regular rotation.
I can guess to a bee-line just what questions are
coming to me next day; and, — if you sit next
to me, on the right hand side, in the Anglo-Saxon
class — by glancing in my book, I can tell you,
to a die, just what question will come to you to-
morrow."

In this one unfortunate respect, the noble and
sincere Dakotah West was without a conscience.
But, if she had had any doubt of Dick's continued
affection, it was now dismissed by the manner in
which that young lady arose and embraced her.

"*I* shall take up Anglo-Saxon," said Dick.
" And I'll sit next to you, Dakotah, on the right
hand side."

So Dick's elective course at the University of
the Three Lakes was made to consist of Botany
and Anglo-Saxon.   On the following day she went
up with Dakotah to the charming recitation-room,
on the fourth floor of the rotunda.   There, these
two beautiful and lamentably ignorant creatures
seated themselves modestly by the rear windows,
through which they gazed out contented upon the
enchanting view, frequently conversing with each

other in subdued tones; or they sought out diligently, amidst a maze of matter, the questions which should come to them later in the Anglo-Saxon class; or made plans for that large part of the day which should be unbroken by recitations; or watched with cheerful interest the progress of immediate events, as when a low murmur of amusement ran through the room, while the teacher of Botany stood demonstrating a floral design on the blackboard with an ace or a knave of some color pinned fantastically to his coat-tails.

The Anglo-Saxon class was composed of a rather more select and enlightened company, but through the midst of this mental respectability, Dick and Dakotah, exercising a caution worthy of a far better cause, steered their dark craft with phenomenal success.

Professor Dane was indeed surprised that Dick, a new pupil, unacquainted with Anglo-Saxon, should show such sudden aptness in appropriating that dead language. At her fluent recitation his kind, dark eyes rested upon her with pleasure and approval. That noble, unsuspecting look set Dick's wild and sinful, but not utterly depraved nature, in a tumult. A longing, something of the old Dyms-

bury Park impulse, came over her then and there
to declare fearlessly that the recitation was an
unscrupulous fraud ; but the sudden shame died out,
and the easy, reckless good nature came in.

A pair of large green eyes, in a head that
reclined comfortably against the wall at one end of
the class semi-circle, which eyes had been constantly observing Dick, noted the signs of this
brief spiritual struggle with a smile.

A little note found its way down the line : —

" DEAR MISS WEST : —

" Please introduce me to your friend, and oblige,

"Yours, etc., D. GAYLORD."

" He comes from our place, and it's a splendid
family, and he's the richest boy in school, and his
father allows him to keep two horses here, and he
has a sail-boat all his own," Dakotah rapidly
whispered.

It was the enumeration of his last two excellent
qualities that gave Dick's heart a sense of kindly
emotion towards Daniel Gaylord. " Are they nice
horses ?" she whispered to Dakotah.

" Awfully fast !" breathed Dakotah, in return.

While Professor Dane earnestly explained to his
class the derivation of a single Anglo-Saxon word,

Mr. Daniel Gaylord had obtained a polite introduction, by all the paraphernalia of letter, to Miss Dick Bodurtha, and the two had exchanged, across the room, a smiling and conventional nod of recognition.

The professor having explained another word, during which the acquaintance had full time to ripen and mature, another note found its way down the line : —

"DEAR MISS BODURTHA : —

" May I have the pleasure of your company, drive and sail, this P.M. ? South gate, university grounds, 2.30. Shall be highly delighted and flattered. An immediate reply will greatly oblige,

" Yours, etc.,   D. GAYLORD."

Dick waited until the recitation-hour was nearly through, without looking at Gaylord, though quite conscious of the fact that those unblinking green orbs had not turned meantime from their contemplation of her face. Then she turned her own beautiful, laughing eyes to his for an instant, with a dainty nod of acceptance. The green eyes swallowed that pleasing glance with a gleam of gratification, and then returned to their glaring unmitigated stare.

"He's odd," Dakotah whispered, "but he's

solid.   He's literally *struck* with you.   He hasn't lifted his eyes from your face!"

Dakotah was much impressed by the philosophical manner in which Dick recognized so important a conquest.

At the close of the hour, and the dismissal of the class, a few serious-minded pupils gathered about the professor's chair with their text-books and various unanswered questions.   Chancing to glance up from conversation with these, as Dick passed out with the rest, Professor Dane's eyes fell upon the new pupil, and the same look of kindly encouragement and approval he had given her before rested on her for an instant.   Instantly the glow of angry shame sprang up again in Dick's heart, and in the childish unreasoning of the moment she met the good professor's accidental glance with a flash of live defiance and resentment.   The professor turned to his questioners with a bewildered air.   The incident slipped temporarily from his mind.   Afterwards, when it occurred to him, amidst a host of graver thoughts as he sat alone, he was constrained to murmur absently, that "that was a very singular, incomprehensible girl."   But Dick recovered from her warmth to endure the still deeper sting of feeling that she had made herself ridiculous, and with charming consistency she was still inclined to lay the fault at the door of the unconscious Professor Dane; inasmuch, at least, as he had suddenly become the object of her righteous aversion and dislike. Dick ran down the stairs, into the "cloak-room," without waiting for Dakotah West, and now indeed occasion was quick to minister to her wounded vanity.

"Let *me* carry your books, Miss Bodurtha." It was the voice of a youth who stood waiting at the door, the one youth whom Dick had secretly admired in the Anglo-Saxon class, whose hair had a wilful part, whose eyes seemed at once clear with the dew of childhood and melting with expression, and whose red lips were petulantly curved.

"*I* am not rich, Miss Bodurtha," he said, as Dick hesitated; "*I* have no horses, *I* have no sailboat,"—the pleading eyes seemed to melt in Dick's face, the red lips seemed actually to quiver — Dick held out her books without a word, save for a low, compassionate "Thank you."

The conversation of the two as they walked on together was as *naïve* as possibly could be. Indeed the brave youth seemed to Dick as a companion-cherub, whom she had known and left somewhere on childhood's shores and now come back to find in a fuller guileless growth. The full-grown cherub's garments sustained him in his declaration of poverty ; notwithstanding which, he had an air of superior worth and could not restrain even a slight swagger in his gait. "I heard your name, in class," said he, "and I shall never forget it. It is Bodurtha."

"Well, I remembered yours," Dick confessed. "It is Furnival."

"Michael Furnival," replied the youth, "and I am of Irish descent. They call me Furnival, simply."

Dick was moved to ask a simple question, very strange to her lips. "Are you an orphan ?" she said.

"I am," replied Furnival, with a deeply pathetic look in his expressive eyes; "and so are you," he added, earnestly regarding Dick.

"Yes," said Dick, " I am." And if Furnival had then given her his hand to swing in silent sympathy, as they went down the walk together, it would have seemed the most natural thing in the world.

" Do you learn *all* of your lesson ? " Dick presently asked.

" Certainly," said Furnival ; "it is nothing for *me* to learn. Take this book, please. It is a new study I'm going to take up. I've never looked into it. Now turn to any page and read a paragraph. Close the book and hear me repeat it after you."

Dick read a tolerably long paragraph and closed the book. Quick as thought the unattractive and prosaical utterances of the text-book fell, word for word, from the ruby lips of Michael Furnival. Dick read a longer paragraph. It was repeated with an equally astonishing glibness. Dick thought of Dakotah's despair under the circumstances. A gleam of superior amusement shone in Furnival's eyes.

" I presume I could do it if I should try," said Dick.

" Wouldn't you like to try ? " said Furnival.

" No," said Dick, with dignity. " I don't care to."

" I took all the prizes in the Kirkville high school," Furnival continued, ingenuously. " Some of the ladies of the Baptist society came in to examinations,

and they thought it was a pity I should not have
an academical education. I hadn't a cent of my
own, but they insisted on sending me to college
themselves. I've only been here two years, and I
have to take up some of the senior studies already
to kill time. Then they expect to send me to a theological school. They want me to be a minister."

"What sort of a minister?" said Dick, unconsciously admitting a little awe into her conversation.

"Oh, a Baptist, of course!" said Furnival, with
a slight blush.

They had reached the ladies' hall, and Furnival
handed Dick her books, and lifted his hat. "Yes,
I am a pensioner of charity," said the soft, be-
seeching eyes. "*I* have no horses. *I* have no sail-
boat. Farewell, beautiful girl, whom I admire. Am
I not indeed unfortunate? Farewell!" Through
this deliberate and eloquent speech the lips uttered
not a word.

But as the shabbily-dressed, incipient Baptist
minister disappeared down the walk, still comport-
ing himself, in the midst of dark misfortune, with
his airy, irrepressible swagger, Dick watched him
admiringly, and a glow of romantic earnestness

triumphed in her breast. " Perhaps you are poor and being educated on charity! and perhaps you haven't any boats or horses ! " said Dick to herself ; "and perhaps I couldn't ever care for anybody! and perhaps, some time — you need not be a horrid Baptist minister, after all ! "

Dick ate her dinner, dressed, resumed her gay and worldly habit of soul as well, and went to the "south gate " to meet Daniel Gaylord.

The custom of making appointments at the south gate was an established one at the University of the Three Lakes, and was really done in consideration for the feelings of the excellent matron of the Ladies' Hall, whom, amiable and beloved by all as she was, it seemed a pity to harass with so many little questions of an unimportant social nature. A front gate permission, when asked for, was readily obtained, but in view of a considerable number of engagements and acquaintances, matters were greatly facilitated by taking an innocent walk to this retired part of the university grounds, and there assuming the cheerful accompaniment of a beau.

A dulcet-speaking couple were already walking off, arm-in-arm, as Dick approached, and Gaylord was waiting with a light buggy and a handsome pair of bays.

Dick found Gaylord quite as unconventional and more abrupt than Michael Furnival, and wondered if it was the usual interesting habit of the Western youths.

Gaylord's genius seemed to lie in doing one thing at a time with the greatest possible intensity and dispatch. His intention now evidently was to spurn the four quarters of the earth with his chariot-wheels. Even Dick's wild love of motion was gratified. She knew that she had never driven so fast in her life before. Gaylord sat with his feet braced against the dash, holding the lines tightly in both hands, his attention fixed, earnest and alert, upon his flying steeds. Woods, fences, houses, hills swept by as in a confused dream.

"Stop! for Heaven's sake!" cried Dick, at last, in clear wonder and indignation, "I can't catch my breath."

Gaylord pulled in his horses with a satisfied smile. "They're a pair!" said he, and he tenderly wiped a fleck of foam from the neck of one of them with his whip.

Dick caught her breath and then thought she

would like to go fast again.　She spoke eloquently of the horses.　"Do you like college, Mr. Gaylord?" she said, after a while, to the silent Jehu.

"No," said Gaylord, "I like business."　But he did not for an instant pause nor look up from his fond and admiring contemplation of his horses.

Piqued, Dick leaned back in a retaliative silence. Gaylord was as unconscious of the retribution intended as he was of Dick's displeasure.　But at length he spoke : —

"Miss West is a nice girl."

"What?　I beg pardon," said Dick, quite coolly and lazily, "my thoughts have been wandering."

"Miss West is a nice girl," Gaylord pleasantly responded.

Dick glanced curiously at her strange and preoccupied companion, and her face broke up into smiles in spite of her.　"Why, yes! She's the nicest girl I ever knew," said Dick.

"Well, she's good and substantial, you know," continued Gaylord, rapidly.　"There's nothing of the flirt about her.　When she first came to the university I paid her some attentions.　I took her to drive.　She let me know, first thing, in an easy, incidental sort of way, that she was engaged.

She's a special friend of mine, and frequently drives
with me now. Are *you* engaged?" said Gaylord,
all in the same direct and candid utterance, and
getting up speed again with his horses.

"Dick gasped audibly. "Pardon me," said she;
"my emotions overcame me. No, Mr. Gaylord.
my unplighted affections are still wandering
about, all ready to light on some hapless object."

Gaylord hardly divined the spirit of this wickedly
audacious speech. "I guess that isn't anybody's
fault but yours," the honest youth said, gallantly,

"Thank you," murmured Dick. "Your kindness is not wasted upon an unfeeling heart."

"Oh, well," said Gaylord, tightening his grip on
the reins and bracing himself still more firmly
against the dash, "You're young! But we've all
got to come to it —or, that is, pretty much all of
us —and it's a good thing, too!"

The wind took the words from between his
teeth. Again, trees, fences, houses, all wayside
objects appeared to swim before the flying pair
in giddy confusion. Conversation ceased.

When Gaylord stopped at "Lake Squall," where
his boat was, the university buildings were visible
on a distant eminence. Gaylord secured his horses

and hoisted his sails.   All his motions were silent, amiable, swift.   He was pleased to find a stirring breeze on the lake.   As rapidly as they had before sped over the ground they now galloped over the crested waves.   The sailing was a new experience for Dick.   It exalted her to an earthly paradise. How broad the troubled lake! how green and soundless its depths! how wild its hurrying waves! She learned how to steer the light craft.   She learned where the dangers were.   Her eyes grew solemn and large, her lips parted, the color deepened in her cheeks, and the wind blew her sweet hair in her face.   It was a pure, childlike, natural expression.   It was as fair a face as one could conceive of for an angel; Gaylord was now steadily regarding it.   But Dick, looking out, had become careless and unconscious of his gaze.

"Will you go again to-morrow?" said he, as they neared the end of the course.

Dick turned to him suddenly with enthusiasm, "Oh, I will go whenever you will let me!" said she.

It was perfectly evident that it was not the prospect of again enjoying Gaylord's society which so transported Dick.   But Gaylord smiled confidently

to himself. "This is a sort of business it won't do
to drive *too* fast," he mused. "Girls are so infernal skittish, you've got to exercise a reasonable
amount of moderation."

Dick did not mind the swift and silent drive
home. It was dusk as she hastened up the walk
to the Ladies' Hall. Suddenly, Michael Furnival
stood in her path. As the youth, so ardently
admired a few hours ago, stood before her, Dick
realized with inward horror and dismay how
thoroughly, how completely she had forgotten him.
He moved her almost to contrition by the silent
language of his eyes. With those pleading and
pathetic orbs he informed her that he knew she
had been sailing with the happier possessor of
horses and boats; ay, and that he knew she would
go again. He then, in audible speech, spoke
sadly though fluently of the many restraints and
misfortunes which embittered his life. He spoke
touchingly and with eloquence of the deep experiences of his soul. It seemed a topic of absorbing interest to him, and he besought Dick to linger
yet a few moments at this dim, affecting hour. So
sublime a flow of sentiment formed an interesting
contrast to the caustic speech of Daniel Gaylord.

But, at an unfortunate moment, Dick realized that she was hungry, and she gave Furnival her hand with a melancholy, though abrupt, good-night.

As she entered the hall, the good matron, who chanced to be passing, looked at her with some surprise. Dick approached the matron with a smile and pressed into her hand a parcel of bon-bons which Gaylord had precipitately bestowed upon her at some moment during the swift exploits of the afternoon. The matron playfully pinched Dick's cheek, and bade her be a good girl and passed on. Being late for supper, Dick ran down into the servants' hall and appealed to the sympathies of the cook by the gift of a generous piece of coin, and had a table spread for her with great glory and *éclat.* In her room a box of birthday gifts from aunt and guardian awaited her. There too, in faithful waiting, sat the calm and beloved Dakotah. Dick surveyed her costly gifts critically and without enthusiasm.

"Eighteen years old!" she exclaimed, triumphantly, sitting down on a corner of the bed. "And *now*," she added, with serious warmth, "I hope I shall occasionally be permitted to do as I please!"

CHAPTER XIV.

A PAIR OF HUNGRY EYES.

FROM the south gate to the lakes, — three paths, more or less circuitous, but all familiar to the feet of my Dick Bodurtha, and traversed, during her brief university course, with many a gay companion.   Sometimes it was with Dakotah that Dick went, for there were boats to hire along shore, and Dick was used to the oar ; and the two made long watery voyages of exploration, or rocked idly on the wave.

Occasionally Dick stole down to the shore and enjoyed the sinful, thrilling, secret bliss of going out alone with sails !   Professor Dane's house was among the substantial mansions on the cliff, though Dick knew it not.   Late one afternoon he saw the little, white-winged boat reeling in recklessly among the waves, and, with indignation in his keen eyes, recognized the girlish form of the solitary and adventurous pilot.   He went to the matron of the Ladies' Hall and solemnly warned her.

"It cannot be," said the good matron. "What! that sweet, fastidious creature! and she has not asked me for permission to go sailing, even with a companion, for a week! It must have been one of the village girls. I am sure you are mistaken, Professor Dane."

But on the following day Professor Dane requested Miss Bodurtha to remain after the class. "Did you go out by yourself in a sail-boat yesterday?" he asked, when they were alone. There was no commendation in his eyes now, but the stern, direct question.

In all her life, Dick had never had youth or man look at her before in such severe, uncompromising fashion, — she, the lovely, the adored, the worshipful one! and she stood speechless with wonder.

Professor Dane repeated his question.

Dick's spirit rose to the occasion. An old and energetic asseveration of Dymsbury Park, to the effect that he was troubling himself with affairs not concerning him, flashed through her mind; but she was too full of scorn to wish to appear inelegant.

"I am not in the habit," she replied, loftily, "of

attempting things that I don't know how to accomplish."

The professor did not retreat. Dick knew that his tone, though so firm, was even and kind. "Will you answer my question ?" he said.

At the strange mastery of his voice, his manner, his eyes, the girl's proud spirit made a hasty and desperate avowal of its irresponsibility. " I *did* go out sailing alone," said she; "and, more than that," she added, " I shall go again whenever I choose to do so."

"It was a mad performance," said Professor Dane, " and must not be repeated. I give you seriously to understand, as I would any incautious person whom I should discover in a like perilous situation, that it must not be repeated. If you ever attempt to go out on the lake in that way again, — and if you ever *do* attempt it I shall know it, — I will send immediately to your friends and have you removed from within reach of the danger. We are supposed to be dealing with rational young men and women, and not with reckless children ; but, remember, I shall know if you attempt the thing again, and I shall do at once and to the letter what I have said I will do. I will not detain you longer."

"Indeed!" said Dick, superciliously, defiance and scorn flashing black in her eyes, "your conversation is so interesting I am sorry that I must so soon be deprived of the pleasure of hearing it!"

The professor did not look black nor reply. A look of pain and perplexity crossed his face,— a face that had a quiet air of being set steadfastly and simply in the direction of duty.

As Dick went out she knew that she had not conquered — neither by beauty, nor scorn, nor impudence; but the victor sat within there, in just and manly purpose, unmoved. This unaccustomed consciousness of defeat affected Dick with a painful wonder. She tried in vain to realize and weigh the situation. But she secretly resolved, for one thing, that she would not again go sailing alone on the lake. She had a perfectly sound, though unintelligible conviction that Professor Dane would discover any such attempt : and, furthermore, she did not doubt that, if occasion arose, he would unhesitatingly carry out his threat. Dick was much pleased with the University of the Three Lakes. She enjoyed life there, on the whole, very much, and she had on hand at present many affairs of an important nature which she did not wish summarily disposed of.

Daniel Gaylord and Michael Furnival had now become as old friends, sweetly acknowledged subjects, available to while away the hours on any occasion ; while around the candle of Dick's charms other moths had not been slow to gather. In circles outside the unhappy and disturbing influence of Professor Dane, she was acknowledged to be the most sweet-tempered, the most lovely . and engaging of girls. She found a piquancy and interest in each new acquaintance. She bestowed her gifts freely on the matron, her money on the cook, and in walking, rowing, sailing, and driving, the sunny days passed by.

Even the Anglo-Saxon class was felt, on the whole, to be an aid rather than a hinderance to her pleasures, for it gave a few comparatively calm moments in which to arrange the swelling tide of other affairs. It became a very popular class, and notable additions, especially from among the number of Dick's male acquaintances, were made to it from time to time. Underneath its decorous exterior there went on indeed a busy traffic in notes, choice communications pursuing their adroit and silent way through devious paths. Professor Dane, earnestly preoccupied, was conscious of some annoying, intangible quality at work in his class. Signs of perplexity appeared now and then on his brow, which passed away before the weight of his more serious and positive efforts.

One day the professor having, without warning, assumed what Dakotah West designated as a "vile habit of skipping around," Dick and Dakotah were intellectually overwhelmed by the sudden dark catastrophe. Dakotah's expression was helpless and affecting in the extreme. Dick, too, acknowledged the annoyance, but was engaged in too wide a variety of pursuits to be seriously disturbed by one fatal incident. Receiving, at this moment, a communication from one Charlie Wilson, containing precious words of condolence, coupled with an invitation to drive, she set herself quietly to work to indite a suitable answer. Professor Dane, when once awakened, exercised an uncommonly keen and comprehensive order of vision. He saw the little note, though so cautiously written and minutely folded, and he courteously, though emphatically, requested that there might be no more of this foreign employ in the class.

Five minutes afterwards, supposing, from his preoccupied air, that he had forgotten, and grown bold through too long license, Dick essayed again to send the little note forth on its journey. The mighty Dane beheld and paused. Dick, who had ridden the wild colts of Dymsbury Park and defied all the teachers of Mount Grimrood, turned strangely and instantly pale. Professor Dane, without any exhibition of temper, yet gave a moment of very serious and decisive consideration to the circumstance which had irritated him. Disobeyed by this heedless girl in the presence of all his class, in the same presence he gravely criticized her conduct as captious and inconsiderate, as that, in fact, of a "mere, spoiled, wayward child."

Poor Dick did not throw off the trouble as lightly as was her wont, — she, the brilliant, the fair, the adorable one, unused to savage, or even logical treatment. She sat, with burning eyes, perfectly still and pale. But fiery indignation was visible on the countenances of those her youthful admirers. Gaylord fixed upon the professor green orbs, charged with an unblinking wrath, and Michael Furnival, in the hall, loudly proclaimed his readiness to denounce, to threaten, and to fight. Dick laughed a little insanely.

"You will do nothing of the sort.   He did quite right," she said — "But I *hate* him!" she added, with a convulsive effort that choked her like a sob.

Through the door Dick saw the professor's form bowed at his desk.   She knew that he had heard.   She caught, as in a flash, something of the meaning of his patient, troubled face, of the signs of bitter struggle surviving in his strength, the marks left by early hardness in his knotted hands.   An arrow of shame and remorse went to her heart.   She felt stifled with an indescribable pain.   She longed to get away from Gaylord, from Furnival, even from Dakotah, from all.   In her room, she threw herself impulsively, face downward, on the bed.

Was it true, then, that for all her attractive grace, her praised and winsome ways, she, Dick Bodurtha, at heart was to be only condemned, pitied, and despised?   "Selfish! inconsiderate! a wayward, trifling child!"   She, who had dreamed of so much, — that was long ago, at Dymsbury Park, — so much attainment and goodness for her long long life!   And she had not utterly forgotten, it occurred to her now, sometimes, how, when the new play was over — some time — she meant to be wiser and better than any one else. And the years were passing, and she was losing the way. So many things blinded her. It was *all* a play, — all empty, restless, vain. Dick grasped the bed-clothes in a tearless spasm.

"But I won't like *him*," she concluded, relevantly, rising. "He tries to make me remember with his hateful, compelling eyes. He wants to have me unhappy all the time, I presume. But I shall not be. It *hurts* me to like him!" cried Dick, fiercely, "and I never, never will! I said that I hated him, and I do!"

So Dick was as happy and light-hearted as ever for several days, and, when her mind was compelled to revert to the subject, she ardently hated Professor Dane.

Following the time of almost unbroken clear weather, there came at length a week of drenching rain. The paths of pleasure became floods of water. The south gate stood dripping and desolate. In the tediousness within doors, and general dearth of entertainment, Dakotah West suggested to Dick that they should put on their water-proofs and go up to the usual Thursday evening service in the chapel. In taking advantage of this idea

both had a mournful, though unspoken, consciousness that they were reduced to a condition of
almost pathetic straits.

The president of the university, who usually
presided on such occasions, was absent. In his
chair Dick saw, with singular emotions, the form of
the odious and dreaded Dane.

Impelled, doubtless, by motives similar to their
own, Dick and Dakotah observed in the assembled
company a number of familiar and despondent
friends with whom attendance at Thursday evening
chapel was not habitual. A casual observer would
have noticed that the brow of gloom lifted, in some
cases, as these two favorite young ladies entered
and religiously seated themselves in an inconspic-
uous part of the room. Ample opportunity for
flirtation arose. Dakotah enjoyed the social atmosphere, though she sat nobly attentive to the
discourse. Dick desired not to listen, nor even to
have the appearance of listening. She intended
to comport herself with quiet decency, but she
had not come to the chapel to hear words from the
lips of one who had despised and wounded her.
With sublime indifference she turned her face and
her thoughts to the contemplation of other things.

The good Dakotah listened and heard not. Dick persistently closed her ears, and wherever she looked, or into whatever widely-wandering channel directed her mind, even through a long dialogue of the eyes, exchanged with Daniel Gaylord, in which the weather was mutually execrated and the dear, idle sail-boat regretted and better hope expressed for the future, she heard distinctly, and distinctly understood, every utterance of Professor Dane's.

It was not a sanctimonious voice that spoke; it had no conventional pulpit tones — but it was like the story of a soldier bearing real scars from the battle-field; or of a pilgrim worn and tried. It touched the hidden springs of life, and the unknown depth and sorrow of Dick's heart responded. From listening and determining not to listen, she consented at last to listen; and still putting up invisible hands to ward off the disquiet which harassed and distracted her, she seemed to hear again, in the tones of that gentle and persistent voice, the flute-note that stole up from the meadow where poor Job Trench had laid his martyred head. Was the grass long on his grave? Dick wondered. Were the flowers still growing there?

The old, sweet meadows, — she would like to throw herself down in them, with her heart to the earth. What other mother had she known! She heard again the plaintive flute-note. She heard the solemn and jubilant trumpet-peal that swept over the hills, after the hard self-denial of another brave heart; all the voices of Dymsbury Park rising, like the wind, pure and free, calling to simple life and greatness of soul and some true and noble work.

Dick listened to them with the old childish eagerness. She guessed something of their meaning now. Who could tell her the rest and deepest? Who could tell her what they said to *her?* The good man talking there. He, though following in a widely different path, had heard them and learned all their mystery.

Dick forgot her rancor and dislike, forgot everything personal, except that she was troubled and that there seemed to be the key; she vaguely longed for help, and there breathed a strong and benign helper. Upborne, for the time, by this new and purely spiritual excitement, she purposely stole away, while Dakotah lingered to speak with a friend after the service, and hid herself in the crowd, avoiding Gaylord, too, who thought she had passed out.

Professor Dane had turned to the organ and was touching the keys thoughtfully. He supposed the chapel quite deserted, when this erring and incomprehensible member of his class stood suddenly before him, her face pale, her eyes unnaturally large and bright. Dick met the professor's surprised gaze without shrinking or embarrassment, speaking in an unconsciously eager tone :—

"You told me what you thought of me the other day, Professor Dane," said Dick. "In class, you remember, you told me what I *am*. I know it — very often — as well as you. But you ought not to have told me that unless you can tell me the other, what should any one *do*? What should any one do in *my* case?"

In those bright, tearless eyes there was a look that startled the good Dane, — beautiful eyes, he had seen them only full of mischievous and laughing glances. They touched him now with their strangely spiritual expression, a deep, honest, almost pitiful soul-craving. He saw and bowed his head with unspeakable kindness and compassion ; and, desiring to answer truly, he moved the organ-keys to a strain that so rose from struggle to glorious rest and strength, that, in the exalted moment, Dick's passionate soul understood and was satisfied.

When the professor looked up, his strange guest had disappeared, — but not the hungry eyes. They haunted him for hours afterwards — pathetic ghosts ! with their wonderfully deep expression.

CHAPTER XV.

DICK MAKES A CONCESSION.

DICK lay awake for full a quarter of an hour after she had got home from chapel, and, in the course of such severe and unseasonable meditations, she concluded that if she was going to set about her own reform in earnest, she should begin by apologizing to Professor Dane on the morrow.

"Let me see," said Dick, drowsily counting on her fingers in the dark, "there are *three* things; — a — a — *saucing* him about the sail-boat — and — — a — a — *snubbing* him in class — and — a — a — —," but sleep came to the relief of that already overtaxed spiritual organization, and soft fingers and pathetic eyes and murmuring lips all yielded to sweet repose.

But that Dick should have entertained the idea of apologizing to the Dane, signified more of an awakened conscience than one would at first suppose; for my lass, though she may have had deep moments of contrition, had ever refrained from any soft acknowledgment of them,—the lingering stoicism of Dymsbury Park, where, if one did another an injury, he should in due time make practical amends, but the admission in sentimental speech that one could be in the wrong was considered imbecile and weak.

It was the more strange then, that, as the morning rose bright and fair, and Dick calmly thought over the triumphs and escapades which should adorn the new day, her soul was full, at the same time, of a most sweet and grateful consciousness of repentance, and her apology seemed the crowning art of the hour.

When Dick looked "good," she somehow looked more than that. Dakotah called it "entrancingly divine." Yet it was not guile; it was not artifice. It seemed, with my Dick, a sort of rare and exquisite inspiration; it seized her mightily; it breathed from every pore of her sweet and freshly dressed body; and it would have convinced the most hardened sceptic.

Gaylord watched her in class, and marvelled and admired, and afar back now in his consciousness slumbered the thought that "girls are infernal skittish."

Furnival watched her, and longed to draw forth from her, in some dim and melancholy light, the history of her soul's new experience.

And still Dick breathed forth sweetness and repentance.

She made another complete failure in her recitation, but one would as soon have thought of remarking the fact in the case of some heavenly alighted guest, whose mind, unfamiliar with Anglo-Saxon, was yet redolent of angelic lore.

And when her school-mates had passed out, Dick leaned both white arms lightly on the professor's desk, and the look in those deep, clear eyes of hers was intoxicating to mortal sight.

"I am sorry, Professor Dane," said Dick, "that I spoke so rudely about — about sailing, you remember. And I am sorry that I was so rude in class — and I hope you will excuse me."

"Why, as for your going out in the sail-boat alone," said Professor Dane, quickly and pleasantly; "you know how to manage it a little, but you don't know how to manage it very well; and the lake is an unquiet body at best, and storms come over it very suddenly, — and therefore, as far as that is concerned, I am glad that you are sorry.

And, for the other, it is of no consequence.   It is quite forgotten.   You are fond of sailing, Miss Bodurtha ?"

Dick gave a little sigh and cast down her eyes. It signified, that although her heart had once found pleasure in such vain conceits — and, in truth, Gaylord's boat was to be ready, by agreement, at three o'clock of that very afternoon — she now seemed to herself to be absorbed in all heavenly meditations and desires.

Down by the cliff on which his dwelling stood, Professor Dane had a strong boat of his own. Whether he would have cared to give this rare penitent a sail in it or not, his honest heart certainly warmed over her with great kindness.

"I suppose I've been too fond of pleasure of all kinds," said my inspired Dick, tracing a fine pathway through the dust on the professor's desk with one delicate finger.

"Perhaps the Anglo-Saxon bothers you.   Is there any fresh trouble with it ?" said Professor Dane, awakened by the girl's pensive manner to an almost tender sympathy.

At this, blush after blush chased each other over the velvet of the penitent's fair cheek ; for had not her discomfiture in class been occasioned by the professor's new habit of "skipping around!"

Dick did not, however, weakly confess to this crime. In such case it would have been necessary to implicate Dakotah; besides she reflected, that, with a conscience now so dangerously on the alert, it was necessary to pause somewhere, and she wisely concluded to draw the line here.

"Why," said she, with delicious evasion, and lifting her eyes gently to the professor's face; "do I have such *very* poor lessons?"

The professor longed to say "No." He longed to comfort that sorrowing young heart; but more than all else, he was honest.

"I am afraid," he said, in a thoughtfully compassionate tone, "that they have not been very good lately. But I think that that can be improved. Perhaps I can help you —— "

Here the sedate army of the professor's senior Latin class came filing into the room, and Dick murmured softly, "Thank you, Professor Dane;" and her eyes fell again for an instant, and the sweet blush mantled her cheek, and she picked up her unworn Anglo-Saxon text-book and departed.

But in her very next solitary moment, Dick

beat her hands upon her breast, after a light affectation of the manner of those who display their towering emotions on the stage. "He isn't like any of the rest; he's more fun," said Dick, "than Furnival and Gaylord and all the rest put together! But, somehow," she added, carefully arranging an eyelash in the glass, "I know I never could *like* him in the world."

Dick's periods of inspired goodness were variable in their duration. In the present instance the palm of purity and peace seemed to have taken up permanent abode upon her serene and lovely features. And now she and Dakotah tried to devise some way in which, under Professor Dane's new method of class procedure, they might make a tolerable shift at Anglo-Saxon without yet committing the whole lesson to memory.

During the pains of these deliberations, and while as yet no master-stroke of policy had yielded to their struggling genius, they had themselves excused from class for three consecutive days by professed reason of severe and disabling headaches.

On the afternoon of the third day, as Dick, surrounded by a laughing group of the university youths, was cooling her aching brow in a retired and pleasant part of the university grounds, she was startled to see the brave Dane himself, swinging his arms in a rapid advance down this secluded path, which afforded him, indeed, a shorter cut home to his high tower on the cliff.

Dick's forehead, though supposed to be racked with internal pains, had, it must be confessed, externally, a singularly tranquil and untroubled appearance. The first cloud which had visited it for some hours now appeared, as she became aware of the professor's approach, in a becoming little knot of perplexity, which knitted itself between her eyes.

"Disperse!" she murmured in a low tone to her companions. "Depart! abscond! quietly scatter yourselves, until these calamities be overpast!"

It chanced that Dick had this day been carrying her Anglo-Saxon grammar about with her with a politic view to effect, and as she now opened its unfamiliar pages and bent her eyes upon the obscure text, the little knot of perplexity on her brow deepened to an expression of almost acute distress.

She wondered whether the professor would

merely lift his hat and pass by, or stop to speak with her a moment. He stopped, surprised at meeting her there, and with such real faith in her indisposition, and such real pity for her suffering softening the gaze of his keen dark eyes, that the conscience, which really did repose somewhere in Dick's fair being, rose up in hot rebellion, as it had frequently done before in this presence. "I never thought of it as anything *wrong* before," Dick thought; "why should *he* always make me feel so, and always makes me feel guilty? But, guilty or no guilty," Dick continued firmly to herself, "don't you dare to blush the way you did the other day in class, Dick Bodurtha, *or you'll get pins stuck into you when you get home !*"

Buoyed up by the prospect of so desperate an alternative, Dick nerved herself to meet the professor's gaze bravely.

"You should not bother yourself with the book if you are ill," said Professor Dane. "Put it by and enjoy the pleasant weather."

"Oh, I do," said Dick, in answer to the last suggestion ; and, "I — I haven't a great deal," she stammered, helplessly, in answer to the first.

"Professor Dane, I really don't know *how* to

learn that book," said Dick, after a moment's pause, lifting her beautiful, piteous eyes to his face.

"Don't know how!" said the professor. He took the book. It was tiresome standing. He looked about him.

Would he sit down with her — with her, poor, ignorant, conscience-smitten Dick Bodurtha, in this delightful place! He laid a fallen bough across two heaps of shrubbery. "Let us sit down," he said, "you must be tired."

"You are too kind, Professor Dane," said Dick, and she knew that that was all too true. She sat down on the bough and the professor seated himself beside her.

Dick knew that her scattered companions were watching her in astonishment from various points well removed. She fancied that she caught the gleam of Gaylord's emerald eyes from behind a distant pine, and she distinctly saw Furnival gazing upon the wondrous scene from afar. She did not call the professor's attention to these objects.

Dick knew, but she cared not, for her soul was happy. Why she was so happy she did not inquire. Extreme bliss, indeed, seemed this sweet creature's natural and rightful atmosphere ; and as she sat on the same bough with the professor, looking over the same book, with the same sunbeam glancing through the branches from her eyes to his, Dick coddled herself up in her wonderful, unquestioning content, and was inspired with a tenfold goodness.

Why it was that the ever ill-treated Anglo-Saxon grammar so soon found its way out of sight and out of mind, slipping quietly down, down on to the very ground, I cannot tell; but there it reposed in fluttering ignominy, yes, at the good professor's feet.

And why it was that Dick was moved to reveal so much — truthfully, without thinking whether it was truth, confidingly, with only a wondering sense of something sweet in the confidence — of her past life to Professor Dane; even of Dymsbury Park, and of Excelluna, too, in whom the professor took a particular interest, asking Dick if she wrote to her frequently — and Dick felt sorry and confessed that she had not for a long, long time, and the professor said he should think, if she would, it would please the poor lonely woman, and Dick blushed, in spite of the prospective pins, and said she had just been thinking that she would write her a letter that very night —

And why the professor found so much, from his own sturdier experience, to mate with and console this pretty confidence, laughing sometimes with a hearty gleam in his eyes, sometimes listening or speaking with a grave and helpful strength —

Why the Anglo-Saxon grammar should have fallen to the earth and all this come about I cannot say. But when the sun at last had gone down completely over the lake in the west, and a chill breath of evening came up in the air, my Dick and the professor looked up with a mutual impulse of surprise at such swift and erratic performances on the part of Dame Nature.

" I have kept you too long," said the professor ; and he rose and picked up the despised little book which my poor Dick, alas ! was never to learn how to study, and he walked back with her along the frequented path past the feminine eyes at the windows, to the door of the Ladies' Hall. There he took the girl's hand for an instant in a firm, kind grasp as he bade her good-night, and entered after her, and courteously apologized to the matron for her absence. Professor Dane was evidently unacquainted with the less pretentious formula of the south gate.

Dick.went to her room with the air of one walking in a blissful, half-incredulous dream. But among the feminine gazers at the window, one pair of eyes had kindled with a little foretaste of mischief. Dick had walked, as if still happily dreaming, to the glass, and stood there unconsciously arranging a few scattered locks of hair.

"So you've got another victim," said a giggling voice at the door. "What a mighty, mighty fish this time, Bodurtha!"

In plain truth Dick was not partial to her feminine acquaintances, always with the one exception of the beloved Dakotah. In the case of the present base intruder, she took no pains to conceal her indifference.

"Well, Kidds," said she, without turning her face from the glass, "if you have any errand state it."

What "Kidds" had started with the intention of stating for something like what it was, a mere vague hypothesis, she was now piqued into affirming as an incontestable fact.

"Prepare to pick up your heart," said the sharply giggling voice. "But of course you ought to know, what everybody thinks, the learned and mighty Dane might go around with you a little just for pity, to try and convert you, but he's engaged to a Miss Lawrence that lives in this place; and she graduated at the university, and she's awfully smart, too, and didn't use to stay out of class, I guess, because she couldn't learn her lessons!"

Kidds could not see Dick's face in the glass. Dick watched it herself with a sickening dread and wonder, paling, paling quite to the lips. Dick was used to taking her own time for answering unpleasant girls. When she did speak it was the clear, cool voice of the Dick Bodurtha whom Kidds knew.

"My circle of acquaintances is not so small," said Dick, " nor my knowledge of society so infinitesimal, nor my desire to immolate myself at the altar so great, that I am in the habit of regarding every man who speaks to me as a possible husband. Will you kindly enter and close the door, or depart, my dear, as you see fit."

"I know a good many who say it would *look* better if you went more with the girls, anyway," said Kidds, forcibly closing the door from the outside.

Dick remained standing still for a moment or two, then she went to the door and quietly locked it.

"After all," said Dick, looking up at last with those tearless, pathetic eyes from where she had thrown herself in an attitude of abandonment by the bedside; "it's a great deal better as it is. I've said I always wanted to be perfectly free, and I do. It's a great deal easier and happier not to care, and I'm afraid, if I'd kept on, I might — I *might* have liked him."

At a small reception which the young ladies held in the parlors that evening none was gayer, there was none whose eyes shone so fearlessly bright as my Dick's. But those bright eyes, if one had known the truth, saw through a dreary maze, and the lights in the room, and the faces of her companions, and the stars when she caught glimpses of them through the windows, seemed to be paling, paling.

CHAPTER XVI.

A TROUBLED LAKE.

THE angel of goodness departed. The restless demons came back with increased power to take possession of Dick's heart. At the University of the Three Lakes this was the girl who cared for nobody and who dared everything; whose eyes mocked you, whose sweet laugh had caught an unpleasant ring.

The matron of the Ladies' Hall having been made aware of several bold indiscretions on Dick's part, took an opportunity at last gently to remonstrate with her. Dick lifted her eyes to the matron's face for an instant with such a weary, almost haggard look in them, that the good woman was disconcerted, and if Dick was not mad for pleasure, then she knew not what ailed the girl.

"What should you advise me to do then?" said Dick, speaking lightly. "It is no more trouble to you than it is to me. One must fill the time somehow."

To this considerate and respectful speech the matron replied, with a face full of wonder; "I don't know what ails you, my child," she said.

The good Dane was troubled, distressed. He looked in vain to see once more the hungry expression, or the heavenly aspiring expression which had seemed to him to open like wells, giving glimpses of an unknown depth. If he chanced to meet Dick's eye, it was only a surface glance that she vouchsafed him — brief, indifferent, heedless. Yet Professor Dane judged far more truly and deeply than the matron. He knew that it was not purely increased happiness which gave the wilder gayety to Dick's manner. So delicately he divined her condition he knew that any stern or reproachful word would fall like added fuel on some already desperate and mysterious despair in that young heart. She had forgotten the hour of her sweet, strange confidence in him; otherwise it seemed to him that he might in a metaphorical sort of sense have taken the sorrowful young creature in his arms and asked her to tell him the trouble.

The professor having dismissed his last class, rose and gathered up for later perusal the written exercises which some of his senior pupils had left on his desk. In doing so he detected one scrap which appeared to have fallen from among the others to the floor, and he picked it up and hastily thrust it into his pocket with the rest. At ten o'clock that night, looking up from his books, and the pleasant fire burning in his grate, which latter seemed doubly cheerful in contrast with the storm which had risen and was blowing outside, he bethought him that he would now examine those class exercises. He spread them out on his table, — neatly written and correct they were, — disquisitions in Latin on learned and abstruse themes. The professor smiled a little proudly at the progress through which he had watched those ambitious pupils. When lo ! in the midst of the dignified array, there suddenly arose before his eyes, and seemed to grow, as he gazed, into gigantic letters, a ragged, pitiable little scrawl indited in the most reckless English. Even before he had formed any idea of the contents, or glanced at the signature, his heart thrilled with a subtle sense of the writer.

"Dear Furnival," said the note; " I go to please myself. I've always wanted to explore Little Squall Island by moonlight. Do you, reverend sir, have the boat ready by eight o'clock sharp. Won't we sail home fast by the pale, pale moonlight! And the cook — she is my dearest friend — she will for me unlocketh the window.

> "Thusly ever of theely,
>
> "DICK BODURTHA."

And the girl who had planned and written this was the one who had told him a few short days ago, with such a divine grace of expression, that she was "sorry!" Furnival had accidentally dropped the communication while passing out of the class-room, and it was this that he had picked up, supposing it to be one of the Latin exercises.

These things flashed through the professor's mind without his heed as he looked out through the night and storm to see the white caps breaking on Lake Squall.

Of one thing he was terribly, instinctively sure — for it had been pleasant at the time the two had planned to start — somewhere out on that dolorous lake, or under its senseless waters — "O my God!" said the professor, shuddering — or, perchance, chilled and drenched with the wind and rain on that shelterless little island, was Dick Bodurtha, her only companion a slight and bookish

Adonis, whose knowledge of sea-craft was hardly equal to the girl's own.

The professor, usually inclined to meet every emergency with the best of courage and hope, now made ready for his battle with the elements with a set face, hopelessly. If they had reached the island before the storm arose, as was possible, "the lad" would advise staying there, he thought; "but the girl! who could tell? Great heavens! she feared nothing."

He passed out through the room where his sister, a woman dressed in widow's black, with a face as strongly refined as the professor's own, was folding away her sewing. In answer to her look of surprise, he told her the story briefly.

"There's no hope," he said; "the girl is insane, and the lad is a puppy with soft sinews."

An intense nervous energy escaped him with these last syllables. The sharp, unusual bitterness of the Dane's tone surprised his sister most. He, hastening down the narrow cliff-path, so familiar that his feet bounded over it, even in the dark, with the utmost firmness, was conscious neither of wind nor rain. He dragged out his boat alone; the boat that was the jest of sunny days, with its cum-

bersome, unwieldy strength. The toughness of
the oars well matched the rower's strength. He
held it against wind and wave, firmly, desperately;
the look in his face which sets doom and tempest
at defiance. He was toiling towards the island.
There was one hope. "One hope," the professor
muttered over to himself. Had he too gone insane, because that one hope seemed suddenly to
absorb all his life, past, present, and future? She
had tacitly appealed to him. Perhaps he could
have saved her ! Or did he dream that, if perchance one golden head had gone down beneath
the wave, whatever triumph or joy might come to
him in later years there could never be any bliss
for him like the bliss that might have been !

As the toiler neared the island it was midnight.
There was no cessation of the wind, which blew
colder, but the moon shone out through a rift in
the clouds, and there in that pale light, on that
desolate, melancholy shore, to the angry swash of
the waves and the shrill moan of the wind, were
revealed my Dick and Furnival dancing ! Verily,
it was done to keep the breath of life in their
drenched and shivering bodies. And "Verily, I
thank God !" said the professor, heeding not while

he beheld them : and not until long afterwards the scene came up to him as possessing something solemnly, ludicrously weird.

Furnival hailed him with a shout. But my poor Dick ! she would rather have shivered and danced through the night than that this man who loved not her should come to save her for his great pity. Ay, she believed that she would rather have died, and gone to sleep down under those sombre waves. Her hair hung loose and wet about her, her garments, too, were soaked and dripping with rain ; and it seemed to the professor, if this fair girl had lived many sorrowful years, she could hardly have turned to him eyes of a deeper misery. But those lovely, miserable eyes did not fill nor shrink.

"Furnival did not fasten the boat securely ; the storm came on us unawares and we lost it," said she, calmly : "otherwise I should have ventured to go home with it."

"I do not doubt it," said the professor, gently, as to some sick or irresponsible person. The tone springing from the deep kindness of his heart, Dick could not understand, save as dictated by sublime contempt and pity.

"I shall not trouble you," she said ; and then

the light and the misery both seemed to fade out
of her eyes, and she sank down all in her golden
hair and her drenched garments in a dead, weary
faint.

Furnival thought it was death indeed, and his
expression was intensely, unaffectedly tragic.

"Good-bye, Professor," said he, waving his
hand. "God knows we meant no harm. I am
going to drown myself."

Between the two the professor had a hard time
of it. He succeeded in capturing Furnival and
bringing him to reason ; and he lifted the unconscious girl and bore her to the boat. There he
wrapped his coat about her and made as comfortable a place for her head as he could ; she gasped
several times and opened her eyes to misery again,
but lay perfectly still as he had placed her, only
putting up an arm before her quiet face.

The wind and wave being on his side now, the
professor made for the shore rapidly. He heroic-
ally accepted Furnival's Lilliputian efforts at help-
ing him haul in the boat, and spoke to him with a
manly consideration which touched and won Furnival's heart for all time.

"Don't imagine it's all your fault, my lad," said

he. "Cheer up. Run home and get in between some dry sheets—and learn wisdom for the future. My sister will care for this young lady."

"I can walk home," said Dick, vainly endeavoring to brace her chilled and weary members against the wind. "The—the cook will let me in."

"Oh, I don't see how you can!" exclaimed Furnival, ruefully. "It's a mile to the hall, and you look so, and you fainted dead away over on the island."

But the professor had already deliberately taken Dick up in his arms and was carrying her up the cliff towards the high tower. Furnival turned to look a moment, before he struck out for home.

"Never mind," said he, a little bitterly. "He deserves her. Let him have her. I've got my precious skin and bones."

Borne up the hill in the professor's arms, saved by one who despised her, carried to his house a shivering burden for pity's sake, Dick's proud heart bled and broke. "My sister will care for her," he had said. Dick thought of the girl who had giggled out those heartless word-arrows at her door; and this unknown sister of the professor's, might she not be more unkind? She had good reason to be unkind.   She would be vexed because her brother had been called out to toil through the storm at night to save a heedless girl. She would show a silent contempt for and suspicion of her. She would attend to her wants with something of the kindness one might show a suffering dog.

At the door Dick caught her struggling breath.

"You must put me down, here," she said; "I will *not* go in there. I am so miserable, it doesn't much matter, I know, but I cannot and I will not bear that."

"Will not bear what?" said the professor, with grave wonder. "I should think you might trust me, child, at least. My own dear sister is not more honored and sacred in my thoughts than you shall be in my house to-night."

"Oh, it isn't that!" moaned Dick. "I *do* trust you, and I know you'll be good and kind. And I wouldn't mind a whole army of wild Hottentots," said poor, tired Dick, desperately. "No, I wouldn't! For I believe they might pity me and be good to me; but I'd rather *die*, yes, I'd rather lie right down here on the doorsteps and *die* than go in there as I am now, and meet a *girl!*"

In spite of the solemnity of the occasion a smile played under the professor's moustache.

"My sister once had a daughter," said he, "who, if she had lived, would be older than you are now. She is not a girl, she is a true, sympathetic woman. And our only maid-servant is over forty years old, and is at present, I have no doubt, peacefully slumbering away in the attic. Such terrors were all in your imagination. Dismiss them. Come."

But Dick could not smile. "I don't much care," said she — "but I don't mind going in now." And like some strange, bewildered bird, with spent breath and bedraggled wings, Dick entered into this warmed and lighted home.

Never a question the angel in black asked her, Dick remembered; never a smile at her misery, nor a scowl, nor a mean suspicion, crossed that strong, fine face. But she *understood* — as the immortals do — and fed and warmed and clothed the belated bird and put her in her own sweet room, and, by the very grace of her presence, charmed her into a seventh heaven of rest.

In the morning, before any alarm could have been occasioned by reason of Dick's absence, the good sister accompanied her to the hall. The matron was a gentle friend of the professor's sister, and the latter so tenderly related to her the story of Dick's midnight adventures that the matron only rose and clasped Dick enthusiastically to her breast. "You must rest. You shall not go to your recitations for two days," she said.

"Isn't it strange how I get out of scrapes, now that I don't care anything about it!" mused Dick, with a sad, impersonal interest in the case, as she wended her way to her room. She found Dakotah there, gazing blankly at the untumbled bed. But, if the matron had been moved to clasp Dick to her breast, what were Dakotah's emotions on hearing the tale of her darling's exploits. She too remained away from recitations, and ever and anon gazed at her friend, as though she saw her restored to her from the dead. As for Dick, she smiled and talked bravely; but it seemed as though her life *had* slipped away somehow.

The matron having proscribed intellectual toils for Dick for the present, my lass engaged with Dakotah in a game of chess. Here, having arranged their hostile forces, they carried on battle with such a vagueness of manœuvre and with such an artless generosity of conduct, the one towards the other, that victory forgot its laurels and defeat was robbed of its sharpest pang.

Still later Dick wandered down to the matron's room. The matron made her lie down on the lounge in her pleasant sitting-room, showed her her scrap-books and photograph-albums, and chatted to her entertainingly. While there, there came a ring at the hall door. The maid brought in a card, — " For Miss Bodurtha, " — and the name on the card was Erwin Dane.

" He might at least leave me in peace," thought Dick ; but her heart did not beat violently, nor her eyes shrink in the straight gaze she had fixed on the matron's face.

" I will go into the reception-room and see him," she said.

" No, no," said the matron. " It is too chill for you there. You shall have this room in which to receive him. I am going out."

Before Dick realized that the matron had passed out, or recovered herself to lift her head from the pillows the matron had placed for her on the lounge, the professor had entered the room. So she took advantage of the needed support the pillows gave her, and lay still on them. The professor had never seen her look so pale and **lovely.**

"It s very kind of you to come to inquire for me," said Dick; and further than that, though she was not embarrassed, she seemed scarcely to care to meet the professor's eyes.

The professor spoke pleasantly on a variety of ordinary topics; and then, as it was so still and they were alone together in the room, he approached a subject nearer his heart.

"When I was rowing out there in the storm to find you, last night," said he, "I thought over many things. I made up my mind that I would never again allow any conventionality, or any — any feeling whatever of my own, to prevent me from offering my whole heart's assistance to one who might seem to need my aid — who might seem to need the aid of any honest and friendly heart."

Dick, growing paler and paler, looked away and said nothing.

"I am so much older than you — my experience of life has been so much different — I have a right to speak to you thus. And I thought — once," — continued the professor, his deep voice trembling, "that you regarded me as one whom you might trust. Once I fancied — and I shall never forget it — that you looked at me as though you believed

I might indeed have some power to help you. If you knew what I would give to help you — if you knew —— "

Alas, poor Dick! She saw this not as love but magnanimity, a magnanimity that stung and slew her.

"Stop!" she cried, impetuously, putting up her hands before her eyes, while a deep red spot of agony and shame glowed on either cheek — "Stop! I do not want to hear you! I cannot bear it!"

"We will let that pass then," said the professor, gently, his own face very pale. "But for God's sake, my poor child," — he said, with a quiet disregard for his own suffering — "tell me what troubles you?"

Dick kept her hands over her eyes. She could not hide the flaming cheeks. "I'd rather die," said she, through her white teeth; "I'd rather be flayed — and quartered — and — and quartered *alive!*" cried poor Dick, with a desperate recollection of Excelluna's book of martyrs — "than tell you!"

"Am I indeed so poor a comforter?" said the Dane, sadly, smiling a little in spite of all at Dick's ghastly hyperbole of speech.

"If you wanted to be kind to me," Dick went on, excitedly, "you would leave me, you would never speak to me in that way again. I am tired, I can not bear to hear it."

"Well," said the professor, still gently, rising, "I can be kind to you in that way. When you are calmer you will appreciate what I have said at least enough to know that I am always ready to serve you. I beg of you that you will never let any — anything *false* prevent you from giving me that consolation, if I can help you." And he was gone.

Dick lay motionless, covering her eyes, until all the color had faded slowly out of her face again. Were those bright eyes never to know tears? She lifted them with a burning despair. The tears were unutterable in the child's heart — ah, if Dick could have known, it was not Miss Lawrence, however learned and admirable she might be, whom Professor Dane loved, but this wretched, wretched little girl with the suffering, tearless eyes.

CHAPTER XVII.

THE "STARRING" TOUR.

THE term was near its close at the University of the Three Lakes, and my Dick and Dakotah were glad; for they both felt that the star of their intellectual course was waning, and needed rekindling amid other scenes.

Dick being too far removed from her friends in one direction, and Dakotah in another, to make it practicable that they should return home for the short vacation, they both accepted the invitation of Dakotah's aunt, who lived in the suburbs of a lively western town about fifty miles distant, to spend the time with her.

There, amid ample grounds, and with saddle-horses at their disposal, it may truly be said that they enjoyed a season of complete mental rest.

Early in the course of the vacation, Gaylord, having paid his dutiful respects to his parents at home, came to sojourn in the town where

Dick and Dakotah were, and rode with them daily.

The trio became interested in the affairs of the liberal church with which Dakotah's aunt was connected, in so much that they planned a theatrical entertainment for its emolument. They found a play admirably adapted to their force of execution; Dick was the intractable and capricious; Dakotah, the calm and matronly; Gaylord, the practical man of fortune; but for the gay and dashing adventurer — who could suit save our gifted Furnival? So a letter, with money for the journey, was sent to the poor but beauteous youth at "Kirkville," whither he had gone to rejoin his supporters amongst the ladies of the Baptist church, with his pockets full of prize-medals and certificates of high college advancement and commendatory letters. Furnival quickly responded to the call, and the cast of characters was complete.

And many miles away, Mrs. Bodurtha and Mr. Higgins, who had conscientiously removed their charge "from within hearing distance" of the allurements and devices of the theatre, slept the unawakened sleep of the just.

"Victims of Fashion" was brought out on

temporary boards in the vestry of the liberal church at B——, and was received with unbounded favor, and, in truth, the amateur performance had something extraordinary about it; for while Dakotah and Gaylord did their part creditably, Furnival developed a sudden astonishing genius for the art, and my Dick, who had a rightfully inherited *penchant* in that line, threw into it the concentrated force of a restless and feverish will.

The repetition of the play was thrice demanded in B——. The last time it was given in the town concert-hall, on a spacious stage, with a flattering number of supernumeraries, and under the fairest auspices in every way. The success was brilliant and unprecedented. The local newspapers appeared with such headings as "The Coming Dramatists," "High Art in High Circles," "The Sensation of the Day," etc., etc.

None took these laurels more to heart than Gaylord and Dakotah. Astounded by the sudden revelation of dramatic brilliancy in themselves, the noble-minded pair became a prey to glorious ambition; while Dick and Furnival cleared all obstructions from the stream with characteristic impetuosity.

A " starring " tour through some of the Western towns was planned for the remaining two weeks of the vacation. The proceeds were to be devoted to completing Furnival's education, his relations to the ladies of the Baptist society in Kirkville being regarded somewhat in the light of an ignominy. It was the aim of the unstudious three of the company to relieve their gifted companion from sectarian and impecunious restraints, and give his illustrious genius room to follow some more congenial bent. If the starring tour should prove a failure, pecuniarily, it was only a more exciting way of travelling; the rich three had money enough with them, and Furnival should still be the object of their tender consideration. But, as sometimes happens in cases where there is a gay spirit of unconcern and no hampering need, the adventurers sailed on in a wonderfully smooth and remunerative course. Gaylord advertised their coming through successive towns, in posters of exaggerated size, blazing with letters of red and gold. They occupied the most elegant rooms in the hotels, and had the natural air of haughty and distinguished worldlings. They were even *fêted*; on one occasion invited to dine with the Mayor of Peak City.

Hence it was that the last week of the vacation passed by, and the University of the Three Lakes opened its doors again and gathered in its scattered flock from the North and the East, and the South and the West, but witnessed not the return of our gayly starring adventurers. The latter left letters and telegrams behind them. They did not regard themselves as runaways, but they knew that the time must now be short ere they should be overtaken and arrested in their triumphant career. This gave all that was needed to complete the piquancy and charm of each mad day.

And during these days Dakotah was perplexed by something in Dick's manner. While that young lady entered into the play with an apparently absorbing enthusiasm, trilling out her stage laughs with an undeniable clearness and flavor, Dakotah noticed in her conduct at other times a singular gentleness and an unaccustomed consideration for the wishes and moods of others. Now the majestic Dakotah, as we know, attributed the ever even-running of the great world's wheels to *love* — and I fear that her conception of love was largely bounded by the emotions of her honest heart toward Harry Fortune. Be that as it may, she immediately concluded, and rightly, for aught I know in this case, that Dick's milder nature had been awakened by the magical touch of an earthly affection. She was strengthened in this belief by the astonishing patience with which Dick now listened to her glowing and heartfelt confidences. She believed that Dick had accepted Gaylord.

So, lingering a little in Dick's room one night — "I am glad, dearest Towhead," said Dakotah, with startling irrelevancy to the theme they had just been discussing — "and I *know* you will be happy. You shan't say a word to me about it until you please. I'm just as glad as I can be for both of you — but, oh, Dick," she went on, in a tenderly bantering tone — "think of the mighty slain! And if you'd only been content with boys, but you brought down such a *man*, such a great big man, Dick darling! Oh, I'm positively sure of it. I allude to Professor Dane. The mark of the fatal arrow was unmistakable. I saw; and then I watched him, you know. I shall never forget how he used to look at you in class sometimes. I could forgive him anything until he began to skip around. But that poor man loved you desperately, — why, Dick! Dick *Bodurtha!*" exclaimed Dakotah, rising, with an accent of wonder and dismay, "What makes you look so *deathly* pale?"

"I'm tired," said Dick, shivering nervously. Dick was in bed. Dakotah went to her and put both warm arms around her. It made Dick think of the first time Dakotah had taken her into those comforting arms. Dakotah had a way of meeting and encompassing unknown troubles with an all-pervading sympathy.

"Now, of *whom* were you speaking?" said Dick, presently, when recovered, with a careless air of trying to remember which did vast credit to her powers as an actress.

"I was speaking of Professor Dane," said Dakotah, looking at Dick with great directness.

Dick fearlessly returned the gaze. "And you said you thought he was in love with me," said she.

"I know it," said Dakotah. "I could see it, and so did everybody else that had eyes."

"But you see you were mistaken for once, my dear," said Dick, rather slowly for so much lightness as she meant to convey in the tone. "He was engaged to Miss Lawrence. Kidds told me so."

"Kidds lied, then," said Dakotah, with unhesitating simplicity of expression. "Miss Lawrence was always *trying* to catch him, but she couldn't, and Kidds was positively *demented* over him, and she saw that he liked you, and so she told you that!"

"Oh, well," said Dick, wearily, in the gentlest tone one could conceive of, while never a tear came for help to her eyes; "it isn't of much consequence to us either way, my Dakotah. I am a great bother to you, Dakotah. Kiss me goodnight."

Dakotah silently kissed Dick, though in a manner that conveyed a world of meaning, and left her. Outside she paused, and her tragic and unwitnessed action was inimitable. "I see! I see it all!" said Dakotah, in pantomimic gestures. "It's perfectly overwhelming! Oh, that devilish little Kidds! How I would love to shake her. But who would ever have dreamed of it! And there's something excruciatingly divine about it, too." Dakotah closed her lips with an emotion and resolve too great for further expression, and proceeded on her way.

Dakotah was as considerate of Dick's proud nature as a mother might be of a child. Yet she could not help shedding silent tears at times when she watched the girl next day; all the more for the unfaltering lightness and gayety of Dick's manner.

But somehow the exhilaration had all gone out of the play for the majestic and matronly member of the company, Dakotah. Her part, to which, though faithfully studied, she had ever been obliged to lend large powers of improvisation, now escaped her utterly. In a helpless manner her mind wandered. She cared not how soon the end came now.

The end was not far off. That very day came a letter to Dakotah — and how came any blow to the beloved Dakotah but delightfully!—a letter from her father, advising her that if she would leave her strange wanderings and come home to him immediately, *immediately*, she should have the desire of her heart; she should have Harry Fortune for a husband and he would accept him as a son.

Now Dakotah, who walked by faith, though so majestically, rather than by any habit of acute penetration, and who, though she had not feared the end, had by no means anticipated this, immediately conceived of herself as having carried on an exceedingly shrewd and brilliant line of policy.

"Did you ever see anything like it — how *beau-tifully* I've brought pa 'round?" said she, in a tone of elated confidence, to Dick.   Then, in the midst of her own happiness, another thought came across her, and she looked toward her friend with an impulsive longing and with tears shining in her eyes.   "Oh, my poor, sweet darling!" she exclaimed, softly,

Dick deftly avoided the tender apology, and Dakotah wisely returned to the happy recital of her own affairs, delighted at finding Dick, in spite of all, such a cheerful and sympathetic listener.

But there could be no doubt that in Dakotah's case the call of love had proved superior to the more exalted claim of art.   The starring tour was at an end.   It was at an end, indeed.   Later in the day a card was brought to Miss Bodurtha — the "Hon. B. J. Higgins."

Dick met her guardian in the hotel parlors.   He was smiling, affable — congratulated her on her charming appearance, and, in soft, laughing tones, on her brilliant theatrical success.   He regretted that he could not see the performance, but his affairs made it imperatively necessary for him to start for home on the morrow.   Of course she would be ready to accompany him. "At nine o'clock in the morning, my dear. Good-night."

Gaylord met Dick as she came out. "Smash-up?" said he, interrogatively, thrusting his hands in his pockets.

"A smash-up," Dick assented.

"Complete, eh?" said Gaylord.

"A very complete smash-up," said Dick, who liked this odd, honest friend of hers immensely.

"When are *you* flying?" said Gaylord.

"To-morrow morning," said Dick.

Gaylord puckered his mouth in a long, noiseless whistle. "I've enjoyed this thing," said he; "but I took it up just for a recreation, a gallop, you know. I've had my gallop and now I am all ready to jump off."

"I think that's the way we all feel about it," said Dick—"only we shall be separated so far. Dakotah and I are not going back to school. We are going to our homes, ever and ever so far away from each other, and from the Three Lakes."

Gaylord fixed his mouth in another noiseless whistle. "One thing I thought of when we set out on this expedition," he said, "was that I should like to get acquainted with you particularly.

I thought if we liked each other we might get engaged on this trip. I like *you* confoundedly, but I've watched girls enough to know that whoever you're likely to think of, in a marrying sense, you know—it ain't *me*."

"I *do* like you, my good friend," said Dick earnestly, "with all my heart. But no," she added quietly, "I never shall marry. I never shall marry anybody."

"Nonsense!" said Gaylord, laughing. "That'll make a capital joke on you sometime," he continued, reflectively, as if laying it up in his memory. "But we've all got to come to it, that is, pretty nearly all, and it's the best thing. I mean to get through with this college nonsense, and marry sometime before a great while, and when I get a home of my own, I bet a box of gloves you'll come with another fellow to see me some time."

The "company" sat late in their private parlor that night, over their farewell talk. Gaylord put his mind to it and made a business of talking. He was practical and hopeful for all.

Since he had heard of the new course events were taking Furnival had said little. He sat on an ottoman at Dick's feet. While the others planned and talked, his head fell back gradually and rested against Dick's knees. She stroked his hair with as purely thoughtful a caress as a sister might give a brother.

Gaylord watched the action. Amidst the haste and excitement of getting off in the morning he drew Dick aside for a moment. " Don't you ever worry about Furnival," said he. " I shall keep an eye on him. They'll take me back at the University, and if they take me, they shall him. He shall go through college and have a good chance afterwards."

Dick gave Gaylord her hand for gratitude. She looked him frankly in the eyes. Gaylord knew then that, whoever Dick was likely to think of "in a marrying sense," it was not Furnival.

At the leave-taking with Dakotah, Dick was impressed by something mysterious and determined in that noble creature's conduct, and which bore her up under circumstances, where, otherwise, her ardent and affectionate nature would have been dissolved in a torrent of tears. The last glimpse Dick had of her she was still standing, pale and composed, with an unspeakable resolve imprinted on her firmly closed lips.

Dick listened to her garrulous guardian without any attempt to conceal her weariness or her dejection. Only once, when he intimated that his influence would prove sufficient to shield her wholly from her aunt's natural displeasure, Dick gave vent to an expression of such sublime scorn for such championship and such displeasure, as amused him mightily.

Poor Dick! the clattering car-wheels did not make noise enough, nor drive fast enough, to drown the tumult in her heart and brain. Away! away! from the last bitter entanglement in life's distracting play. What next awaited her? So young, and yet to believe it all an old, aimless story. Away! away! ever farther away from the sunny lakes which had opened like mysterious heaven and love to her, only now forever to repeat their restless storm surges in her heart. Ever farther away — as if, after so many miles, she might forget.

CHAPTER XVIII.

NEVER had Mrs. Bodurtha been so kind to her wandering niece. The starring tour, one would naturally suppose, must have dealt her a consummate blow ; yet there was no reproach, aversion, nor despair in her manner.

This caused Dick to reason busily and not without some ground for suspicion. She wondered what new plan had been settled upon for the disposal of so desperate a character as herself; whether she was, indeed, to be returned to the native heathen, or immured in a convent. or sent to a lunatic asylum, labelled as dangerous and a candidate for the strait-jacket, so tenderly and almost enthusiastically affectionate had her aunt's manner become toward her of late, and so adulatory and fond the conduct of her guardian. When the calm secret of these two was disclosed, Dick regarded them as smiling fiends, and the convent or the strait-jacket as tolerable in comparison.

As for her occupation in these days, Dick danced. Mrs. Bodurtha and Mr. Higgins had no notion of making a temporary penitent or recluse of their prodigal; their attempts in that direction had ever met with such a fatal result. The story of her last digression was known in the distinguished circles in which they moved, but it was not incompatible even with Mrs. Bodurtha's sense of truth and justice, which smacked considerably of religion, that Dick's grace and beauty should well carry off her misdemeanors in the eyes of a discerning world; while the guardian insisted that a quality of sweet iniquity in so charming a subject was positively indispensable.

So the end being devised and assured in the minds of the two, they gave the butterfly, meanwhile, a sumptuous field in which to flutter and dazzle. It was the beginning of the gay season. The society in which Dick so freely dallied through the prestige afforded by her guardian was notably of the opulent, banqueting, ball-giving sort. Dick dazzled, feasted, sipped her wine, danced—danced as though a light and careless heart were in every radiant motion; rose late, and dressed, and banqueted, and danced again. The aunt and guardian smiled at this tireless dancer for pleasure's sake. My poor Dick danced more tirelessly than one who dances for pleasure. She danced to forget.

One festive night the doors of the guardian's great house on the avenue were thrown open to the world's elect. It was an affair of memorable lustre and magnificence, a dream of splendor—the lofty luxurious rooms, the brilliant lights, strains of gay, sensuous music, the glitter of gold and silver plate, the noiseless waiting of many servants, the breath of tropical fruit and flowers.

In the midst of the worldly elect, a shining mark for envious or admiring eyes ; in the midst of the gay waltzers, most courted ; in motion most inspiring of all, with a flush on her cheeks and a brightness too fitful in her eyes, Dick danced. Her laugh, peculiar, heedless, but sweetly modulated, when it crept out in the room made a sensation for circles round. Her aunt watched her with secret, unalloyed delight and approval. It was even a satisfaction to her to think, that, whatever hinderances they had met with hitherto in the training of their charge, she had now no objections to offer to her wise guardian's plans in the shape of a heart.

"It used to trouble me," Mrs. Bodurtha mused —"the girl's heartlessness—but we cannot expect deep emotion in the young, and it has, at least, prevented her from running into any ludicrous love fancies. It is excellent, on the whole. When her guardian proposes to her, she may be a little startled at first; but, as he states the case to her, she will at once see its wisdom and appropriateness. She will accept her good fortune and settle down in life."

Mrs. Bodurtha gazed at the unbounded splendor shortly to be laid at the feet of the careless waltzer there in its midst, and a sigh escaped her, express- ive of relief and of gratitude to Providence, who, from so hopeless a beginning, had brought about such satisfactory and distinguished results.

In a pause of the music, the smiling and gracious lord of these stately halls drew near to his young ward.

"Ah, you must rest a moment," he said. "Come and see my mountain of roses yonder. Ah," he murmured, as Dick put her hand in his arm, "it is my desire to make your life always, *always* summer, my dear."

"Don't," said Dick, laughing, shortly, flushed

and breathless, "I should die, I should suffo-
cate."

"Not if you would learn to rest," said the bland
guardian. "Not if you would throw off all your
young doubt and impatience and disquietude upon
an older heart, and be content—well," said the
guardian, smiling, "be content with all that the
world can give you."

Dick forgot her fear for an instant, and gazed
directly at her guardian. The guardian, amusedly
conscious of the piquancy of the stare, kept his
composed face half-turned away from her.

"Do you not admire my fragrant little Hima-
laya?" he said, as they stood amid the bower of
roses. "It happens to be quiet here. I shall not
detain you but a moment. I have concluded, my
dear, that I am not competent to be your guardian.
I endeavored to wield the reins of authority with
great discretion and firmness, and how lamentable
my failure is known to none better than to yourself.
I propose, therefore, to submit the reins wholly,
uncomplainingly, and unreservedly to the guidance
of your own sweet hands, claiming only the right
to be your humble and devoted servant henceforth,
I propose, in short, to be your *husband.*"

Dick, replying to the soft sophistry of this address with an ever-increasing wonder and intentness of expression, the guardian continued :—

"I will say briefly at this moment — it is a matter to which I wish you never to give a second thought ; — the property left you by your parents, owing to some business indiscretions on the part of your father just preceding his death, is hardly sufficient, as an independent fortune, for a young lady of your habits and tastes. In short, it is small — quite small. But why do I speak of this? I share no wealth apart from you. My house, my horses, my servants, they are all yours. My undivided fortune lies at your feet. You have simply to accept of it. Your aunt approves of my purpose. I may say indeed," said the guardian, lowering his smooth tone to a whisper of blandishment, "that she waits at this very moment to congratulate me. Shall I wend my steps towards her? You have carried a high hand, my dear," he continued, with a slight accent of hardness. " It is probably the decisive moment in which it is well for you to obey for once. All the rest of your life shall be happy. I am old and profess no sentiment. You, though young, are quite as devoid of it, I fancy. Accept quietly the wise course. It is indeed no trouble. Your life shall have never a care."

The hot color which had faded out of Dick's cheeks as she listened came back to them again. She laughed through her white teeth with a sweet, defiant madness. "So this is what you and my aunt have been planning!" she said. "You do well to try to frighten me. I am so susceptible to that method."

"Oh, no, no!" said the guardian, reassuringly. "Not to frighten you; only to secure, if you would calmly think of it a moment, your welfare and happiness."

"But if I don't like you! If I never, never could care for you so much, do you want me to *marry* you?" said Dick.

"I said I professed no sentiment," replied the guardian, smiling.

"And why — why — do you think *me* so — so inhuman?" cried Dick, in a low tone, passionately.

"Merely a necessity, my dear," calmly replied the voice of soft blandishment; "a necessity in the case of one so beautiful. Do not trouble yourself about it. It is a law of nature and cannot be avoided."

Dick did not hear. Her insulted soul rose with uncontrollable torrent force to quivering lip and flashing eye. "Hush, then!—I *will* tell you," she said. "I *did* care for some one! I care for him now! I *love* him. I love him with all my wretched, worthless heart. He did not think so much of happiness; he would have helped me to be strong and true. But I *should* have been happy with him—oh, whether poor or rich, in comfort or misery, I do not care! If he made me sorry, I should know he was kind. If he put a knife to my throat, I would trust him! Can you realize it? Did he love me? I cannot believe it! He was too good. - If he did once he never could after what happened. But that doesn't help me. I can't forget, and it is killing me! It is killing me! Do you want me to marry *you*, now?"

"So you have had the illusion, too!" said the guardian, soothingly. "And that is a positive relief to me, do you know; for they say, however we are constituted, it possesses us at some time in our lives, and I am glad to know that the worst of yours is over. Attacking you perchance after marriage, and taking some violent and unfortunate direction, it might prove especially troublesome. I assure you, my dear child, the worst stage is over; it will not bore you long. I propose a foreign tour. You shall see some magical islands. You shall buy a castle in Spain, if you choose!— I have not answered your question. Certainly; you interpret my meaning with great acuteness. I desire to have you marry me."

"It would be to me," said Dick, still with towering emotion, "like giving up the last spark of truth and honesty in my heart, the last pure aspiration, the last faith in God, the last — the last hope in my life. It would be to me like stretching myself out on that heap of faint, sickening roses to *die*, body and soul! That is what your *happiness* means to me! I have seen enough to know. It would be horrible stagnation and death! Do you want me to marry you now?"

"Naturally, my dear," said the guardian, smiling, with unruffled temper, "since I have never seen you so beautiful in my life. Your stage air is wonderfully becoming. As I said, the malady is short-lived. It may pass away entirely with this charming confession. I repeat; my untiring devotion and my fortune are yours. Reflect a moment calmly. Shall I go to your aunt, now?"

Dick laughed as she had laughed at first, sweetly, madly. The music of the waltz struck up again. Her partner came towards her. "Wait!" she said, airily, to her guardian "one more waltz! Oh, indeed I will reflect calmly — as calmly as one can who is so *happy*, you know." The low ripple of her voice smote mockingly on his ears. "Wait!" she smiled back at him, as she swept away.

"A perverse little devil, indeed!" he muttered. But he believed the butterfly had been caught in his web, nevertheless. He was suavely content.

Dick's brain swam. She adapted impromptu lines to the swift music as she waltzed. "It is the most wretched and desperate thing I could do. I am wretched and desperate. It is my fate ; I will do it! I may not live long. One could kill herself in the course of a year or two. He can sacrifice me so easily! I will torment him something as he deserves. I will assume that I have affections; I will bestow them where I choose. A short life and a merry one. I can forget, maybe, when I am bad enough. I will go down in billows of luxury."

The guests were departing. Dick had not returned to her guardian. She had seen him conversing smilingly with her aunt. One or two of the older and most intimate acquaintances in the company even hinted their congratulations ere they went away. "Thank you," said Dick, to one worldly and jewelled matron, who was gushingly going through with this ceremony; "I am very happy, I assure you." The mocking bitterness contained in her politely modulated tones, the strange glitter of her eyes, puzzled the matron beyond measure.

"Pardon, miss," said a servant, handing Dick a letter. It was a strange letter to be taken, in the midst of all that glitter and luxury, into so white and soft a hand, — a soiled, unfashionable sheet, bearing an air of long preservation ; a grotesque, faltering, ignorant hand-writing.

"Ever and a darlin' orphing lamb, I cannot write much, for they say as I am a dyin', and the days is short, they say. I care not, ever darlin', I am a dyin' along o' God.

"But I hear you comin' down the walk, and I raise myself up to meet you, and I look, and it's only the dead leaves a drivin' and a whisperin' down the walk.

"But if I should look up, mebbe next day, and *should* see you, ever darlin', comin' down the walk — I ask not for myself, though lovin' unto death, but because my thoughts was troubled concerning you — it seems as though it would make sech a stillness, ever darlin', along the sorrerful road."

The butterfly was fairly caught: "Let her go and see the old servant die, if she wishes," said the guardian. "After all, it is a charming *ruse*." Dick's manner of stating her intention had had a strange and desperately quiet determination about it.

Excelluna looked down the walk at last and *saw* the darling of her heart. Then she lay back smiling, content, upon her bed for many hours. Dick, in her plain, black travelling dress, her hair arranged with religious simplicity, moved noiselessly, thoughtfully, about the room. Excelluna watched her and a look of solemn significance crept over her face.

"It has come," she said.

Dick lifted her bright eyes with a tender, half-smiling inquiry.

"The tonin' up and the tonin' down, as was both thought on, and was both despaired on," said

Excelluna; "they have been accomplished. Somehow, though *how*, unbeknownst, mebbe, to all, they have been accomplished."

Dick laughed softly, though **her** lips quivered: " I am always good with you, Luny, you know."

"It do not appear as though it had been eddication, in a gineral sense, as have done it," said Excelluna; "since all sech as was tried in a gineral way was despaired on. But through wildness and danger, through failin's and wanderin's, somehow it have been accomplished. It have been wonderful accomplished.

"It do appear somehow," Excelluna went on, " to have left a sadness and as of a bein' tired and of a bein' lost (which well I know, havin' suffered them, most darlin' one). But fear not, for, as I have been a lyin' here, in a revelation I have seen——

"In a revelation I have seen," said Excelluna, solemnly. "You will hear the dead leaves rustlin', for the wind a moanin' through 'em—and you will stand watchin' the golding light, afur down in the meadows, where the grass is green and tender as the spring time, darlin' one. You will watch the shinin' road a lyin' there, and a leadin' up beyend the mountings, and beyend. Peace and love and joy

shall come to you, most darlin' one. We are chil-
dern wanderin', but the way shall not be lost.
Fear not. To sech as is given revelations, it is
known; and in a revelation I have seen." Poor
Luny! But she had always wandered in her mind.

Dick was so patient, so womanly-tender, and
thoughtful in that humble sick-room, anticipating
every want of the ancient serving-woman, stroking
so soothingly the poor gray head, her old companions of the dance would scarcely have known
the girl.

It seemed to my poor lass as though a little
surcease had come in the storm, a breathing-space,
mysterious, grateful, sad.

"Nay," she said, in answer to some anxious
remonstrance of Excelluna's, with whom she was
watching through the night, "let me, dear Luny.
You are happy. I have not been so glad, I have
not had such rest for months and months."

As the young girl spoke thus with strange
eagerness, Excelluna lifted her eyes to look at her.
"Do not fear," she said quietly. "In a revelation,
I have seen." She lay back, satisfied, for that
golden hair, the touch of that soft hand, were
heaven to her.

And so the sorrowful mystery of life faded from before Excelluna's eyes.

" It is like as when I have been into some great, grand church in the city," said she, "and have heerd the organ playin', clear and solemn, but mistractful, not bein' understood. And I have listened to them strains, that seemed a wanderin' here and there, and have been troubled. And then at the end, I have heerd it creepin' out, so beautiful, the old tune that I knew. And I have knowed that it was the same tune a runnin' through it all, but my ears was not trained high enough to understand.

" Ever darlin', weak and wanderin' has seemed my life, sad and mistractful, not bein' understood. But now the music creeps down soft and slow. I listen and I cannot cry, most darlin' one, for I have ketched the tune."

As Dick watched, strangely unwearied, through the hours of the night and day, Excelluna's flesh sank swiftly down into the dark valley ; but the brave heart never realized that, nor could have given to it a thought nor a tear.

And, on the third day, awaking from a sleep in which her face had worn a sublime, untroubled expression, and her lips had moved : " Bring to me," she said, "my flowers that I have made—all ; let not one be left."

When she beheld them, she laughed with soft, pitiful disdain. "They must be put by," she said. "I cannot look upon them, darlin' one, by the side of sech flowers as has been revealed. Take them away. They have answered their turn. These things must be put by."

Thus Excelluna had brought to her, one after another, the treasures once pricelessly dear to her heart, and smiled, and put them by.

On the "Book of Martyrs" she laid her hand lightly. "Yis, put it by," she said. "It's only a poor, sorrerful, half-told story! It is not worth recordin' by the side of sech things as is revealed."

"Ever and a darlin' one," said Excelluna, then, with a look of clear solemnity; "have I been a poor, forlorn creetur, without no home nor kin, lonely and wanderin', weepin' and sorrerful, and oft mistracted?"

Dick bowed her head, laying both her hands with unspeakable tenderness on the gaunt palms of the ancient serving-woman.

"Have I been sech?" repeated Excelluna, in

that tone of clear solemnity. "*It is put by. It is forgot, forevermore.* Help me up, most darlin' one."

Dick raised the wasted form up on the pillows. Through her far-offs Excelluna looked towards the hills. But for once those spectacles, those dear mediums of vision, seemed to obstruct her yearning sight. It was the last poor tie, yielded exultantly.

"Put them by!" she softly cried, "*I can see afar off without them!*"

They who look so glad and far as Excelluna looked then come never to the earth again. But then, she did not *die*. My Dick, who sat beside her, says that she never died. Turning for her great-heartedness, in that last supreme moment, to bless the sorrowing head beside her, it was not the lustre of my Dick's golden hair that she saw, but the dawning ripple of waves on an eternal shore.

Dick stood under the elm-trees watching the golden light far down in the meadows. The wind rustled in the dead leaves ; but there the grass was green and tender as the spring-time. She saw, too, the shining road leading towards the

mountains and beyond.   But Dick did not think of
the "revelation."

In the last few days she had lived of life a year
or more.   It seemed to her, in that quiet hour,
that, like Excelluna, she could leave the pitiful past
behind her.

"I will be brave and true," Dick prayed.   "I
will not think of happiness any more.   I will be
obedient to my aunt and guardian, except in that
wicked thing.   I will do anything for them.   I will
live for them; but I will be true to the faith and
goodness in my heart.   If they do not want me
except I do *that*, then," said Dick, "I will try to
take care of myself.   I will work with all my might.
But I will be true ——

"If I could only have known," said Dick,
"whether he cared!   If he could only know that I
am trying — trying for his sake — and though I
have been so bad, I might, in time ——"

Dick trembled, and lifted her eyes to the hills
again.   "Oh, I *will* try," she said.   "I thought,
when *she* died, I should stop thinking so much
about my own happiness.   I can!   I can give it all
up, as she did, and be brave and patient and true."
Dick watched the marvellous roadway fading slowly

in the west. "It is only a little time for any of us," she moaned. But Dick had forgotten the revelation.

Down the path among the elm-trees, one was coming to meet her. It was what meant peace and love and joy in all the world to Dick. It was the Dane coming down that old familiar path at Dymsbury Park.

So intently, in her deep young despair, Dick stood looking away to the west she did not heed the rustling that his feet made in the leaves. But when she turned at last and saw him, the world that she had given up wrapped itself about her in such sudden tumultuous surges of trembling hope and joy; she stood so pale and startled, the vanquished pride in her eyes pleading through a look of such reproach — pleading desperately for compassion, I think she would have fallen. The Dane was compassionate. He caught her. His whispered words of tenderness and love allayed her fears. On his breast, for the pitiless joy that had almost broken her heart my Dick learned how to cry at last.

"He came clear from the setting sun to find me." Thus Dick tells the story, and blushes still, and will laugh for you sweetly as ever, as she says it ; but with a little half-tearful, defiant flash in her eyes that bids you not to ask for more. He *found* her and he kept her forevermore. As boldly as the viking of old, he carried her to his tower by the Three Lakes.

It was long before Mrs. Bodurtha was reconciled. Mr. Higgins smiled as suavely as ever, and ultimately bestowed his fortune upon a more deserving subject. Mrs. Bodurtha's own wealth was great, but the loss of the smiling Crœsus to her family seemed irreparable. But when Dick's husband made a great name in the land — and, among women, there was none more womanly, more gentle, radiant, and beloved than Dick herself, and her young children were bright and beautiful about her — Mrs. Bodurtha gradually inclined to be conciliatory. Finally, she was accustomed to say with great complacency, folding her cold and jewelled hands one over the other, as people spoke admiringly of her niece : —

" Ah, yes ! — *I* was intrusted with her early training, you know. It was a great responsibility, but I have never been sorry that I undertook it." And the good lady gives a long sigh as she surveys the rich gems on her fingers.

Ah, well! Much goes to make up an education. Mrs. Bodurtha, too, had her share. But it is not of that that Dick thinks in the supreme moments of her womanhood's pain or joy — not of the governesses who came to Dymsbury Park, nor of the teachers at Mount Grimrood, nor even of her aunt's discreet instructions. But she hears many voices. They seem to play ever mysteriously around her life, but clearest then — and not least among them, the lonely flute-note sweeping the long grasses in the old meadows at Dymsbury Park, where a poor little heart went bravely to its rest; not least among them, the solemn chant that seemed to fill earth and sky, when Excelluna put her earthly treasures by, and looked beyond the hills to God.

BOSTON STEREOTYPE FOUNDRY,
4 Pearl Street.

Messrs. A. WILLIAMS & CO.'S
LATEST PUBLICATIONS.

Troublesome Children: Their Ups and Downs.

By ONE OF THEM. With ten full-page colored illustrations, and fifteen plain engravings by Francis G. Attwood. 1 vol. Thick oblong quarto. Exquisitely colored covers. Price, $2.50.

*** Being wholly without cant, affectation, or any attempt to enter into the subtleties of religious creeds; the purity, sweetness, and combined tenderness and humor, together with its high moral tone, will give it, too, an entrance into the home of our American firesides in a way suggestive of the welcome accorded to the "Franconia" stories and "Alice's Adventures in Wonderland."

Sly Ballades in Harvard China.

By E. S. M. With many illustrations and in folded paper covers exquisitely designed and colored by Lambert Hollis, after the manner of the famous Paris "Amateur" Series. 1 vol. Small quarto. $1.00.

*** The most dainty collection of charming fancies since Praed, and worthy of the school which has produced such inimitable jeu d'esprit as "The Little Tin Gods on Wheels" and "Rollo's Tour to Cambridge."

Thaddeus Stevens: Commoner.

By E. B. CALLENDER, member of the Massachusetts Bar. One volume, with portrait, handsomely bound in cloth, $1.25.

"This life will be welcomed by all who hold the 'Old Commoner' in affectionate remembrance."—*Watchman and Reflector*.

LONGFELLOW AND EMERSON.
The Massachusetts Historical Society's Memorial Volume.

Containing the addresses and eulogies by Dr. G. E. Ellis, Dr. Oliver Wendell Holmes, Charles E. Norton and others, together with Mr. Emerson's tribute to Thomas Carlyle and his earlier and much-sought-for addresses on Sir Walter Scott and Robert Burns. Illustrated with two full-page portraits in albertype after Mr. Notman's faithful and pleasing photographs of Mr. Longfellow, and Mr. Hawes's celebrated photograph of Mr. Emerson, taken in 1855, so highly prized by collectors. One volume. Quarto. Boards. Uncut. Price, $2.50; or in white vellum, cloth, gilt top, uncut edges, $3.50. Limited edition printed.

The Sewall Papers.

Diary of Samuel Sewall, 1674-1729. Edited by GEO. E. ELLIS, D.D. 3 vols. Large 8vo. With elaborate index. $9.00 *net*.

*** A literal transcript, in type, of the famous diary of Chief Justice Sewall, of Massachusetts, in possession of the Massachusetts Historical Society. As a minute picture of the manners and customs of early colonial days, abounding in wit, humor, and wisdom in the quaintest of English, it has no prototype. The importance of its publication as a discovery can be compared only with the deciphering of the diary of Samuel Pepys, which it fully equals in interest.

The Deserted Ship; a Story of the Atlantic.

By GEORGE CUPPLES, author of "The Green Hand." Handsomely bound in cloth, gilt, extra. 12mo. Illustrated. $1.25.

"In these two absorbing sea stories—"*The Deserted Ship*," and "*Driven to Sea*"—the peril and adventure of a sailor's life are graphically described, its amenities and allurements being skillfully offset by pictures of its hardships and exposures, and the virtues of endurance, fortitude, fidelity, and courage are portrayed with rough and ready, and highly attractive effusiveness."—*Harper's Magazine*.

Fly Fishing in Maine Lakes; or, Camp Life in the Wilderness.

By Maj. CHARLES W. STEVENS, Commander of the Ancient
and Honorable Artillery Company, Boston. With colored
frontispiece of the best killing flies, and rubricated title-page.
Square 12mo. Cloth. 201 pages. $1.25.

"It is written as naturally and unaffectedly as if told over the pipe, around the evening fire, to a circle of brother sportsmen."—*Pittsburgh Telegraph*.

"The book is really very liv ly."—*Cincinnati Commercial*.

Rollo's Journey to Cambridge.

Illustrations and illuminated cover by FRANCIS G. ATTWOOD.
1 vol. Quarto. 50 cents.

⁎ A satire upon Life at Harvard College in the form of a parody upon the famous Rollo Story Books. Printed originally in the Harvard Lampoon, and later compiled with the consent of the editors into a sqaure octavo in paper covers. The cleverness of parody and satire and the familiarity of the subject have made this a most decided hit. Already four editions have been exhausted, and the demand promises to continue as long as Harvard Colle e maintains its influence on surround-ing social life, and humor continues to be an American characteristic.

Bicycle Tour in England and Wales.

By CAPT. SHARPE and A. D. CHANDLER, President of the
Boston Bicycle Club. Illustrated by four large folding maps
and seventeen brightly finished albertype engravings. Small
quarto. Gilt. 164 pages. $2.00.

⁎ The title gives not the slightest idea of the real contents. It is a work of exquisite beauty, displaying rare taste and judgment, laboriously and elaborately executed, which none but an intense devotee of the wheel could have carried out to such an interesting degree.

Southern Rambles: Florida.

By OWEN KNOX. Very profusely illustrated. 150 pages.
Square 12mo. Cloth, $1.00; paper, 50 cents.

⁎ An amusing and satirical account of a Winter's Trip to Florida, filled with laughable incidents, character studies, descriptions of Southern Life, wholly devoid of exaggeration, showing Florida as it struck the author, and not as the interested guide-book-makers endeavor to prove it to be.

Poetical and Prose Writings of Charles Sprague.

New edition, with a steel portrait and a biographical sketch,
12mo. Cloth. 207 pages. $1.50.

New England Interiors.

By ARTHUR LITTLE. A volume of sketches in old New England places. Thick oblong quarto. $5.00.

⁎ "To those far distant, unfamiliar with the nooks and corners of New England, and prone to consider the work of Puritanical colonists noticeable only for its lack of taste, and conspicuous for green blinds and white painted walls, this work will be a revelation."—*Boston Daily Advertiser*.

The Land of Gold.

By GEORGE H. SPURR. A novel founded upon fact. Illustra-
tive of pioneer life in California in '49. 12mo. Cloth. 270
pages. Illustrated. $1.50.

The Homes of our Forefathers.

A selection of the Oldest and most Interesting Buildings Historical Houses, and Noted places in Massachusetts. By EDWIN WHITEFIELD. Quarto. Cloth. $6.00.

*** Third improved and enlarged edition of this valuable and interesting work which is composed entirely of plates, in color, accompanied with descriptions.

The Homes of Our Forefathers. 2nd Part.

Same as above, but embracing the Historical Homes of Rhode Island and Connecticut. By EDWIN WHITEFIELD. 4to. Cloth. $6.00.

Dr. Howell's Family.   Christine's Fortune.

By Mrs. H. B. GOODWIN. New and popular editions in a very attractive style of binding. Each 16mo. Cloth. $1.00.

"Of the merits of them, it is difficult to speak too highly. They are written in a style as near perfection as it is possible to conceive. Better books a parent cannot put into the hands of a son or daughter."—*Watchman.*

Captain Nathan Hale.

An address delivered at Groton, Connecticut, on the Hale Memorial Day, September 7, 1881. By EDWARD EVERETT HALE. Pamphlet. 20 cents.

Peirce's Colonial Lists.

Civil, Military, and Professional Lists of Plymouth and Rhode Island Colonies, comprising Colonial, County, and Town Officers, Clergymen, Physicians, and Lawyers. With extracts from Colonial Laws defining their duties. 1620—1700. By EBENEZER W. PEIRCE, of Freetown, Mass., member of various Historical and Genealogical Societies. 1881. 8vo. 156 pages. Price, $2.00.

Henry Knox Thatcher, Rear Admiral U. S. Navy.

By GEORGE HENRY PREBLE, U. S. N. A pamphlet biography of the late Admiral Thatcher. With steel portrait. Price 50 cents.

Tower. Modern American Bridge Building.

Illustrated. 1 vol. 8vo. Cloth. $1.00.

*** The only work on modern wooden bridges.

Poems of the Pilgrims.

Selected by ZILPHA H. SPOONER. A handsome 12mo. bound in cloth. Bevelled edges. Heavy paper. Gilt edges. Illustrated in photography. The poems, about thirty in number, are selected from Lowell, Holmes, Bryant, Mrs. Sigourney, Mrs. Hemans, and other great writers. Price $2.00.

James A. Garfield. Tributes from Over the Sea.

Being selections from Foreign Testimonials to the late President Garfield. Sm. 4to. 50 cents.

The Labor Question.

The relation of political economy to the labor question. By CARROLL D. WRIGHT, Chief of the Mass. Bureau of Statistics of Labor. 1 vol. Thin 16mo. Cloth. 60 cents.

*** "Col. Wright has discussed the theme in a striking and original manner, and deserves the thanks of the community."—*Boston Traveler.*

A Red Letter Day.

Poems by LUCIUS HARWOOD FOOTE. Handsome cover in entirely original design, the prettiest of the season. Heavy paper. Elegant print. Square 12mo. 112 pages. Cloth. $1.50.

The Sheep Scab.

Its nature, prevention, and cure. A handbook for American Shepherds. By HENRY TEMPLE BROWN. To which is added by request: "The Classification of Wools and their Marketable Values," an address delivered before the Missouri State Wool Growers' Association at Idaho, Mo., April 5, 1882. 1 vol. 12mo. Illustrated. Cloth. 50 cents *net*.

A New Volume of Proverbs.

Sparks from the Philosopher's Stone. By JAMES LENDALL BOSFORD. 1 vol. Square 12mo. Cloth. Red edge. Price, $1.00.

Walking Guide to the Mt. Washington Range.

By WILLIAM H. PICKERING. With large map. Square 16mo. Cloth. Price, 75 cents.

What Our Mothers Make.

A Pamphlet volume of Tried Receipts first issued for the "Little Women's Fair." Very tasty cover. 60 pages. Price, 25 cents.

Cape Cod Folks.

A novel. By SALLY PRATT MCLEAN. With frontispiece by Mitchell, and a charming vignette outline, drawn and engraved by W. J. Dana, showing Cape Cod and the adjacent islands of Nantucket and Martha's Vineyard; the whole tastefully bound in cloth, with unique and elegant cover, designed by L. S. Ipsen, 1 vol. 12mo. 327 pages. $1.50. Eleventh edition.

"There is real power in her characterization. Real eloquence in her account of the uncultivated singing. * * * Real pathos in the vague religious opinions, and the intense religious sentiment of these simple brave people."—*Boston Advertiser*.

"Her description of the provincial traits of this most provincial of all the outlying New England Settlements, are admirable bits of *genre* workmanship."—*Harper's Magazine*.

Love Poems and Sonnets.

By OWEN INNSLY. Limp, white vellum. 185 pages. $1.00. Third edition.

"It is a lovely volume of lovely verses on the loveliest of themes."—*W. R. Alger*.

"It must be confessed, however, that this volume will probably receive nothing but contempt from the admirers of Whitman and Wilde, for with all its strength and passion, it must seem to them basely and despicably pure."—*N. Y. Evening Post*.

"A sense of power still held in reserve fascinates the reader, and through all its changing forms the fervent passion obeys the master's hand."—*Literary World*.

"The contents are sweet, passionate, and plaintive."—*N. Y. Times*.

Driven to Sea; or, The Adventures of Norrie Seton.

By Mrs. GEORGE CUPPLES. Illustrated. Cloth. Full gilt sides. Large 12mo. $1.50. ☞Eleventh thousand.